"How do I look at you?"

"Like you want to touch." She moved forward, her boldness returning when he didn't walk away. And damn it, she'd come this far, there was nothing left of her dignity to lose. So she wasn't just flirty, she was shameless. "And I *do* know how to touch."

"Really?"

She nodded. Hoping her hammering nerves weren't obvious.

He stood like an immovable mountain. In fact, she didn't see any part of him move as he murmured, "Prove it."

Part of her wanted to tell him to go to hell for playing her so hard. But victory surged through her veins, too. Yes, she'd known. She might be a virgin, but that didn't mean she was an idiot. He wanted her.

She got to within kissing distance. But she wasn't going to go for the obvious. Nor was she going to make it that easy for him. Somehow, she was going to make him suffer for this humiliation.

She looked down his body—as freely, boldly, brazenly as he'd looked at her before. Then she stepped closer, angling her head so her face tucked in near his neck—her own neck exposed to him. She blew, very lightly, on the pulse she could see beating madly just beneath his jaw.

He flinched.

With one light finger, she stroked his forearm, feeling the heat of his skin, the tenseness of the muscles beneath it. She moved, licked her lips, then very lightly pressed them against his salty skin.

He stood like a statue. A very hot, breathing hard one.

Possibly the only librarian who got told off herself for talking too much, **NATALIE ANDERSON** decided writing books might be more fun than shelving them— and, boy, is it that! Especially writing romance—it's the realization of a lifetime dream kick-started by many an afternoon spent devouring Grandma's Harlequin romance novels....

She lives in New Zealand, with her husband and four gorgeous-but-exhausting children. Swing by her website anytime—she'd love to hear from you: www.natalie-anderson.com.

FIRST TIME LUCKY?

NATALIE ANDERSON

~ Just a Fling? ~

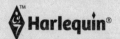

Harlequin®

TORONTO NEW YORK LONDON
AMSTERDAM PARIS SYDNEY HAMBURG
STOCKHOLM ATHENS TOKYO MILAN MADRID
PRAGUE WARSAW BUDAPEST AUCKLAND

Recycling programs
for this product may
not exist in your area.

ISBN-13: 978-0-373-52867-7

FIRST TIME LUCKY?

First North American Publication 2012

Copyright © 2012 by Natalie Anderson

www.Harlequin.com

Printed in U.S.A.

FIRST TIME LUCKY?

For the University of Canterbury's Student Volunteer Army—thanks for showing, in the most fantastic way, that the brightest lights on Christchurch's horizon not only have brains and beauty, but also the most tremendous hearts. You've been such heroes, and you've proved how positive our city's future will be.

CHAPTER ONE

DR GABE Hollingsworth glowered at the bumper sticker on the car in front; the streamlined silver silhouettes reminded him that tomorrow was recruitment day. Half his team would be there to check out the possible additions to the posse of alluring females. But while the players saw the dancers as fresh game, Gabe reckoned the women were the *hunters*, not the hunted, with their sparkling eyes, suggestive poses and PhDs in serious flirting. They might officially 'support' the country's greatest rugby club, but they'd high-kicked more than one man's life right into touch. Including his. So he'd be light years away from the stadium at audition hour tomorrow.

He took the next left, while the silver-stickered car went straight on out of sight. Relieved, Gabe automatically glanced at the property on the edge of the park. He'd been curious so long it had become a habit. So he saw it immediately—the rough bit of board with 'To Let' and a mobile number scrawled on it that hadn't been there this morning. Gabe pulled over and put a hand to his pocket, let it drop again without retrieving his phone. He was right outside—there'd be no harm in walking to the front door and making enquiries in person, would there?

Assuming he could *find* the front door.

A decrepit garage stood on the edge of the footpath while the rest of the front boundary was marked by ferocious planting. He walked the length of the two-metre-high prickly 'hedge' of trees so intertwined you couldn't see through their thick evergreen foliage, then he peered behind the sign precariously tacked in front of the rusted letterbox. He saw hidden there what *could* be a narrow goat track between the branches—make that a single-file ant track. He winced as gnarled twigs scratched his bare arms. Pushing through, he figured it was an abandoned wreck of a house, probably in the midst of some development argument with greenies on one side wanting it to be absorbed into the park, while property tycoons fought on the other for consent to demolish it and put some apartment or office block in its prime central-city location. But the spiky green fortification intrigued him and the idea of having a central-city hideaway appealed given the fatal attraction nightmare his last fling had become. No chance of some unhinged ex-lover carrying out a home invasion here—a high-maintenance type like Diana would never risk her skin and nails to get through. Hell, *he* could barely get through. But he ignored the scratches and catches at his clothing and hair; the resistance made him all the more determined to see what was beyond. He snapped branches and stomped over the rough ground and suddenly was out in open space, blinking in the brightness of the summer evening.

He straightened, forgetting the zillion stinging scrapes on his skin as he stared. It wasn't an abandoned wreck at all.

Roxie only had the downstairs bathroom to do and the place was clean, empty and ready for occupation. She picked up the spray bottle of foul-smelling chemical disinfectant and straightened her sore shoulders. She was determined to get it finished tonight because the optimist in her hoped people might call about renting the house tomorrow. Flicking on the hot tap, she stepped right into the shower cubicle. Getting wet didn't matter because as soon as she was done she'd head to her studio, have a real shower and flop into bed. She hunched down to get into the corners, pointing the jet of water ahead, and furiously wiped the walls. She'd spent most of the day cleaning, had practised her routines as rest breaks to stop herself dwelling on how different the place looked without furniture. It would never be the same now, but would always be home—her heart. This place was all she had left.

She snorted at herself and went overboard with the spray to stave off the OTT melancholic thoughts. The shower was hardly dirty—hadn't been used in months—but she wanted it immaculate, for prospective tenants to see the perfect condition so they'd feel obligated to maintain it just so. Because, much as she didn't want them, she needed tenants. Money of course, so she could finally get on with the rest of her life.

Her eyes burned as she scrubbed. Not from tears—they'd long since dried up. No, it was the pungent fumes of the industrial-strength cleaner setting fire to her senses and not in a good way. She held her breath as she swiped with the sponge but still the acidity swept over her. She shook her head to stop the fuzzy hum, grabbed the shower jet to sluice the suds away more quickly. But the fumes grew overwhelmingly strong. Now, between the suds and the steam and the stench, she could hardly see. She couldn't hear properly either, because over the sound of the running water she thought she could hear someone calling out. But there wasn't anyone here to call for her any more.

Still holding her breath, she stumbled out of the shower, not bothering to turn off the taps, desperate to get to a window because she felt horribly faint.

'Are you okay?'

Roxie jumped, inhaled a last deep breath of chemical vapour and then screamed blue murder. For a method of stopping a faint, there was nothing better. Adrenalin flooded her system in a mad torrent, sharpening her mind and her muscles. Sadly not her vision. She kicked herself for leaving the bottle of cleaner in the shower. She could have used it like pepper spray or something. Instead she was the one temporarily blind. All she knew was some man she could hardly see was in the room with her.

'Hey!' he shouted over the top of her screeches. 'Calm down. I'm not here to hurt you.'

She went silent; the sound of streaming water ceased too. She tried to look but it hurt and she had to squeeze her eyes tight. 'Who are you?' she rasped, her throat raw from her ripped shrieking.

'You've got this stuff in your eyes?'

Roxanna's panicked senses were slightly pacified by the calm question delivered in such a cool, authoritative voice. 'I think the spray mixed with the steam or something,' she wheezed. Not that it was the more pressing point right now.

'It's a wonder you didn't pass out. Here.' He took her upper arm in a firm grip and walked her two paces. 'Sit.' He pushed her down so she was perched on the edge of the bath.

She blinked rapidly, desperate to regain her wits. She heard the tap running in the sink, felt the breeze as the window was opened. But no matter how much she blinked, the stabbing sensation in her eyes didn't ease. All she could see through the fuzzy agony was a tall figure, too close. 'Who are you?'

'Gabe Hollingsworth. I saw the sign and walked right in,' he answered in that same calm voice, but now he sounded as if he was smiling. 'Sorry if I gave you a fright.'

No one 'walked right in'. The hedge saw to that. Most people thought this place was an extension of the park, the gardener's disused cottage or something. She came in through the garage but that was securely locked. So she wasn't sure she believed him. Had he climbed the fence to steal something—or *worse*? But if he was a serial killer or sex offender, would he really be helping her now?

'Your eyes are really sore.' He truly seemed concerned. And, yes, amused.

'No kidding.' She couldn't keep them open they stung so bad. She gripped the edge of the bath with cold fingers and told the rest of herself to chill too. This Gabe guy didn't sound like a serial killer. Not that she knew what a serial killer was supposed to sound like, but she hoped that hint of humour was a good sign.

'We need to wash them out.'

We didn't need to do anything. 'I'm fine. It'll be right in a minute.'

'No, we need to bathe them. Don't worry, I'm a doctor.'

She half snorted. He might not be a serial killer, but she so doubted his ophthalmology qualifications.

'No, really, I am.' He read her sceptical mind. 'Put this over your eyes for a second.'

He pushed a wet and cold folded flannel to her face

and she raised her hand to hold it in place—had to admit it soothed. The taps ran again.

'Lift up.' As if he didn't think she was capable of following instructions, a firm, warm hand cupped her cheek. He took the flannel away and then tilted her face from one side and then to the other as he carefully poured cool, clean water across each eye.

'Try to keep them open,' he murmured. 'It'll help.'

His voice was right by her ear, meaning his face was right by hers. Roxanna's heart thudded. She hadn't been this close to another person in the best part of a year and last time she'd been the one doing the doctoring. This was beyond different. This was—

'Better?' he asked, another too-close murmur.

Goosebumps rippled across her skin as she suppressed a shiver, not that she was at all cold. In fact, she was all of a sudden burning. And all of a sudden she remembered she was only wearing a pair of ancient Lycra shorts and an almost supportive singlet. No bra. While water was trickling down her face and onto her chest. 'I'm getting wet.' She pulled back, wanting to cover up.

'No worse than you already are,' he said, a brisker tone this time.

'I can manage now, really.' She tilted her chin free of his grip. 'Thanks.'

The sting in her eyes truly had eased and she opened them widely to look at the man bent down before her. She blinked more rapidly than she had when they'd been chemical filled. Was she hallucinating her way through this? But no, she'd *felt* his touch, had *heard* his words and now, as her vision cleared, she *saw* him rise to full height.

The effect was something else. Bronzed, broad-shouldered, unbelievable. At least six feet with dark hair and even darker eyes that were gazing right at hers in an uncomfortably intense way. Peripherally she noted the blue jeans, red tee, skate shoes. The cool clothes merely served to emphasise the fit body, the tan, the muscles, the obvious strength that made her glad she was sitting because her knees had weakened from some pathetically female hormone-driven response. And given he had some foliage as decoration, it seemed he really had come through the hedge. But his eyes held her attention hostage—jet-black, bottomless, unwavering eyes.

'Thanks,' she croaked, to break the suddenly dense silence. She swallowed. 'How can I help you anyway?'

He put the glass he'd used beside the sink, then took a few paces backwards, shoving his hands into his jeans pockets. 'I saw the "to let" notice.'

'It only went up this afternoon.' She stood, trying to get some kind of equality in the situation. Fat chance when he was tall and she wasn't. When he was dressed and she all but wasn't. When he was devastatingly good-looking and she definitely wasn't.

'I know.'

'You want to rent this place?' He didn't look like a prospective tenant. He looked like the kind of guy who owned things. Lots of things. Working in retail, even her little-old-ladies-giftstore kind of retail, meant she knew fashionable, what cost lots and what didn't. She knew the watch on his wrist cost lots, so did the shoes, while the tee shirt was one of those priced ten-times too high just because of the label. He was definitely someone who held the cards in his hands.

'I want to buy it,' he said bluntly.

Yeah, definitely the owning kind.

'It's not for sale,' she answered equally bluntly.

He held her gaze for a moment, then dropped to look

at the puddle on the floor between them. 'Where's the owner?'

Roxie's spirit hardened. 'You're looking at her.'

His unfairly long lashes swept up and the deep, dark eyes studied her again—surprise had widened them.

'You don't believe me?' she asked.

'Well, you don't look...' He shook his head. 'Never mind.'

She knew what he'd almost said. He thought she looked too young to own a house? How old did he think she was? Clearly not much older than a schoolgirl. Did he think she was the teen cleaner? Great. But she was no kid, she was twenty-two and she'd cared for this house almost single-handedly for the last five years. Not that she was going to get all indignant and ram that down his throat, no matter how much his assumption annoyed her. And, yeah, underneath that, she smarted because this one-thousand-per-cent man-in-prime didn't see her as a capable adult, or a woman.

The unfairness of the situation riled her. This was her house, but he was standing in her bathroom with the upper hand, having rescued her from a mortifying mo-ment. But she hadn't *needed* rescuing; she'd have been fine. She was always fine. And wasn't it just so typical that the one time in her life she met a spectacularly good-looking man, she had to be looking like a scruffy kid?

If only she had shoes on to give her the slightest chance of looking him straight in the eye—statement shoes, like six-inch stilettos. Instead she had to crane her neck to meet that focused, but depressingly impassive, gaze. She opted not to, instead walked as coolly as she could into the lounge. Not that easy when her heart was hammering faster than when he'd frightened the screams out of her minutes before—he really was something else.

'The house will never be for sale,' she said, aiming for polite but firm. 'I'm sorry you've fought your way through for nothing.'

'Not for nothing.' He followed her. 'I've always been curious about this place. If you don't mind, I'd love to take a look around it.'

She couldn't really say no when he'd just helped her out, albeit in dispassionate passing-medic style. So she nodded and spread her hands wide. 'It's known as the Treehouse. The reason is obvious.'

He walked into the middle of the large room, his gaze raking it with a wide sweep. 'It certainly is,' he said softly.

His obvious appreciation of it helped her forgive him—just a little—for not seeing her as an equal.

'Why are you renting it out?' he asked as he walked closer to inspect some of the detail carved into the picture rail.

'I need the money,' she answered honestly.

'You'd get a swag of money if you sold it.'

'I'm never selling it. I'm not worried about securing a tenant,' she lied.

Those dark eyes studied her again briefly, then his attention shifted to the room's features again. 'It's unique.'

Yeah. It wasn't a modern, floor-to-ceiling windows kind of place. And it wasn't big. Instead it really was a Treehouse—in one corner, an ancient, solid oak grew through the floor—both a support structure and design feature. Light poured in from the cleverly placed skylights, the windows were like frames for the beautiful living landscape of the park. The house itself was all hand-carved, polished wood. Built with the love, sweat and blood of her grandparents and, just as they'd put everything they had into the house, they'd put that same level of time, love and energy into her. Until illness had turned the tables and she'd become the carer for both them and the house. She was never letting it go, but she had to have some adventures now or she'd end up staying for ever and never moving forward. It was time to fly free—but she'd keep the nest to come back to.

'Most people love it,' she answered him. The few people who'd seen it in recent years had. 'My grandfather always said there was nothing like natural beauty.'

The dark gaze rested on her again for another moment. 'He was right.'

Roxie stared back. A frisson of something spiked her goosebumps all the more—he was talking the *house*, right? He'd turned away from her so she could no longer see his eyes—and they were unreadable anyway.

'How long do you want a tenant for?'

'Six-month lease initially, ideally a year,' she spelt out her fantasy. In truth, she'd take what she could get.

He walked to the far corner, where that beautiful gnarled tree literally grew through the floor. But Roxie's attention was totally swallowed by him. His back view was almost as good as the front—the masculine vee of broad shoulders and slim hips reinforced that impression of strength again. She swallowed as heat flushed through her. It was definitely time to move out and explore some of the world—some *men* of the world. She'd clearly been waiting too long when she was this affected by the first she'd come across in ages. He put a palm on the trunk, his fingers smoothing over the bark. She remembered the feel of that palm on the side of her face. Her face now burned.

He turned suddenly. 'I'll sign up for a year.'

Her eyes bugged and she momentarily forgot his hot factor. 'You don't even know what the weekly rent is.'

'Doesn't matter. And I want first right of refusal if you do ever decide to sell it.'

He hadn't even seen the rest of the house, only the living area, but sometimes the house had an almost magical effect on people. For her it was a tranquil sanctuary—though not with him in it, he'd brought in an electrical charge that put her on edge. But she needed a tenant and if he was serious about a year's lease, then she had to get over that edge.

'There are a couple of things you don't know.' She felt it only fair to warn him, even though her heart was pumping even more crazily now with the prospect he was going to solve her financial problems.

'Conditions?'

She nodded. 'You won't have access to the garage or the little flat above the garage.'

His eyes narrowed. 'Someone's in the flat?'

She nodded.

His expression hardened.

'While I'm in town, I'll be living there,' she rushed to explain. It wasn't some random person he'd not met and she'd stay well away from him. Only her explanation didn't make him relax; if anything he tensed all the more.

'You're not usually in town?' he asked sharply.

'I'm going overseas.'

'When?'

'Soon.' As soon as she had the money, but she decided not to mention that getting all the money together was going to take a few months. 'I have some things to do before I go,' she fudged.

He nodded. Eventually. 'Okay.'

Sudden panic slammed into Roxie. It was going to be hard seeing a stranger live here, but it wasn't for ever and it would still be hers—this was the only way of ensuring it would remain hers. She breathed deep and pushed herself on. 'The garden will be maintained by the estate.' That was a plus, right? But she saw his smile of disbelief. 'You haven't seen the garden,' she pointed out defensively.

His hands spread and he looked down. 'I'm wearing half that hedge.'

She frowned at the number of leaves in his hair. 'I hope you didn't damage it.'

'Are you seriously telling me the hedge has a gardener?'

Yeah, he was teasing. And she so wasn't noticing how that smile shot him from hot to sizzling.

'Totally seriously,' she said. 'It needs a lot of care to maintain it.'

'It needs a chainsaw.'

'The hedge stays. As is. That's one non-negotiable condition.'

He walked back towards her, his smile curving his too sensual lips wider and in grave danger of distracting her. 'How am I supposed to get access to the house if I can't come through the hedge or the garage?'

'There's a hidden gate on the park side.'

'A hidden gate?' He chuckled then, an infectious, warm sound.

The surprise of it, the sexiness of it, almost rendered her speechless. She had to clamp her jaw to stop it from dropping, to stop herself drooling on the floor. She pivoted on the spot so she could no longer see him, so she could *think*. 'So much of what makes this house is its privacy. Isn't that what you like about it?'

There was a short silence. 'How astute of you.' No

amusement sounded now. 'All right, those conditions are no problem for me. I still want to rent it for the year.'

Roxie felt more dizzy than when she'd been in the shower accidentally inhaling industrial cleaner. 'I'm going to need references.'

'Sure. How about I give you a cash deposit now to secure it, and we can let our lawyers draw up a lease agreement tomorrow? You have a lawyer, right?'

'Of course. That's her number on the sign out there. I'll get her to put those conditions in writing.'

Gabe nodded and turned to walk back to the tree again, trying to keep his eyes up and away. Because Little Miss Landlady's white vest-top had not retained opacity in the shower-cleaning session. She might as well be topless. But she didn't know that and he didn't want to tell her. He didn't want to think about it a second longer than he already had. No, he didn't want to dwell on how completely gorgeous she was. Instead he lectured himself that she looked about seventeen. As if she'd just walked home from school. And he did not, *not*, not have raging lust for someone barely legal. She was a *kid*.

Except she wasn't. She had the most delicately feminine body he'd ever seen. He'd noticed it at first glance in the bathroom—her long legs, fine-boned shoulders, slender waist, sweetheart-shaped face, smooth, glowing skin, sensually full lips... And then her eyes had opened and stabbed him in the gut. The most vividly blue eyes. He deluded himself that they looked unnaturally vibrant because of that cleaner. That the chemical had some belladonna-poison effect that magnified the intensity of their colour or something. As if. They were just knockout powerful. And now her red-rimmed, stunning eyes were round.

Yeah, he'd have to be blind not to see how she looked

at him. It was a look he was used to and it didn't usually affect him. Only he was working hard not to give her that same look back. That surprised, almost dazed look that had its roots in sensual appreciation and unexpected desire.

Maybe he'd inhaled some poisonous fumes too because he couldn't be thinking this way. Her shorts were old and worn and not any season's style. Her mouse-brown hair was in a bedraggled ponytail that emphasised that schoolgirl impression. And that damn thin white vest-top had gone transparent. He was trying very hard not to think about the pointed peaks jutting towards him. Because he wasn't so out of control as to be turned on by almost visible nipples, by imagining cupping those mounds in his hands and bending before her to kiss the pointed tips, to press his face to the softly curved surrounds.

Okay, he was that out of control and his unruly imagination was making it worse. It'd been too, too long since he'd got laid. Too long he'd been stuck on the straight and narrow and boring. His heart hammered at an insane pace, ringing in his ears. The last thing he'd expected to find beyond that horrendous hedge was an architecturally amazing home complete with some Snow White or Sleeping Beauty or Rapunzel type impossibly pretty Disney princess inside. He couldn't help wondering where the dwarves, beasts or wicked witches were…

Oh, he had to snap out of it. It was just frustration addling his reason. Going for a woman like this—one the same age if not younger than Diana—would be insane. She'd undoubtedly want more than he ever would. She'd be emotionally immature, a dreamer with that happy-ever-after fantasy that he was never buying into. It was when he'd been forced to reiterate that to Diana that her

inner witch had appeared…intense, needy, a knife-edge
to certifiable. Just the thought of that mess was enough
to cool him off.

Almost.

Thank heavens this woebegone waif was heading
overseas. It was only knowing she was leaving that he
could take the place. No doubt she'd return from her trip
all grown up and sophisticated and if serendipity saw
their paths cross again, he'd dally with her then. Uh-huh,
like in five years' time. For now he'd get himself this
hideaway and then hide, right away. In a couple of weeks
the team had that game in Sydney and he was so hitting
the club scene and having a couple of nights all-adult action. Having fought so long to gain independence from
family expectation, he was letting no woman hamper his
freedom. So he definitely wasn't hot for Miss Skinny.

He turned back to face her and named a weekly rental
price he figured should be almost on the money for the
location.

'Actually I'd been thinking a little more than that. My
lawyer will send you the details to set up an automatic
payment.'

So Sleeping Beauty wasn't that sleepy. Good for her
for knowing the high value of her property—and that
he could afford it. Biting back all the flirt talk tingling
on the tip of his tongue, he got his wallet and pulled out
enough cash to cover the first two months. She took it
from him with a steady hand and those wide, wide eyes.

'Don't you think you'd better tell me your name?' he
asked drily, trying to hide how he was dying of desire
inside.

'Roxanna Jones,' she answered, head high and un-
blushing.

'Good doing business with you, Roxanna.' So not thinking about the pleasure of it—of her—at *all*.

'When did you want to move in?' Roxanna gripped the wad of notes tightly to stop herself from touching him and easing her insanely curious fingertips. Since when had her fingertips *itched* like this?

'Tomorrow.'

She gaped. 'You're currently homeless?'

'No, but you were right, I like the privacy of this place.'

'I know.' She smiled, suddenly filled with excitement about her future.

He jerked a nod, turning abruptly away. 'Right, I'd better let you get on and finish.'

'You don't want to see the rest of the house?'

'I'll check it out tomorrow.'

'Okay, once the lawyer thing is done, I'll arrange access for you through the garage so you can get all your stuff in.'

'I'd appreciate that,' he said in a voice loaded with irony.

She tried to slow her out-of-control heartbeat with some sensible thought. The guy was now her tenant meaning she'd better put all her sizzle response in an ice-bucket. Not going to screw up this deal. Soon she'd be free to go overseas and discover all the way hotter guys out there…except she doubted there'd be a hotter male on the whole planet.

'Do you want to go through the gate or back through the hedge?' He hadn't seen the back of the house or the garden, and she wanted to witness his surprise.

'I'll go through the hedge, try to push some of those branches back into place for you.'

'You're sure?' She was disappointed; she'd been looking forward to a smug moment. It was likely to be her one and only with him.

'The hedge is your security system, right?'

Okay, so he was astute as well as gorgeous. 'I guess.' She shrugged as if it didn't matter so much.

'Then I'll cover up the stomping great path I just smashed through it. Wouldn't want anyone else creeping up on you in there and giving you a fright.'

'Good thing I didn't strip off to do the shower, otherwise it might have been you who got the fright.' She giggled, a high embarrassed sound that was embarrassing in itself.

To her surprise, his brief smile seemed as embarrassed and he moved quickly away from her and headed back into the prickly hedge.

Yeah, real clanger. Mortification cooled her right down as she was rudely reminded that Man of the Millennium didn't see her as a woman at all. Shaking her head at her gaucheness, she went back to the bathroom to rinse away the last of the cleaner. She glanced in the mirror and O-M-freaking-G. While her red-rimmed and bloodshot eyes were bad enough, her transparent-when-wet vest-top meant all-out wince city. Somehow the effect seemed more revealing than straight nudity, yet Gabe-the-gorgeous hadn't even blinked. Instead he'd been very particular to look at her face. She figured it had been born from courtesy or something. Or more like utter disinterest given her lack of spectacular in the boobs department. Yeah, that was it. Great. The first mind-blowingly handsome man to cross her path and she hadn't even been able to tempt him into a second look at her near-naked torso. She wondered what she needed to make someone like him do a double take.

She pulled her hair out of its dreary ponytail and

sighed at the straggly mess. No wonder he hadn't blinked. She tousled it with her fingers, imagining a new cut and colour. Then she looked at her chest and mentally fastened a cleavage-creating booster bra. Yeah, it was beyond time to glam up. No doubt the sensible thing would be to put that wad of cash in the bank tomorrow but she'd been without for so long and, damn it, now she had the certainty of a monthly rental income she could splurge, right? Just for once? She'd save all she needed in no time and this way she'd look great for her audition. She'd buy some other things to celebrate with too.

Re-energised, she put her music on and rehearsed one last time—danced hard out until she could dance no more. She slithered to the floor, resting her back against the old tree, and almost immediately thought of *him*. She heard the amused, low voice in her ear, felt the firmness of his touch. Then she remembered his impassive expression and determination seized her anew. No more would she be that *invisible*.

Her work at the Treehouse was finally done; now she deserved some fun. It wasn't just for the audition that she was going to look fabulous—the next time they met, she was so getting a second glance from her hot, built tenant.

Hell, make that a third.

CHAPTER TWO

GABE got to work mid-afternoon, having spent the morning boxing up the few personal possessions he cared enough about and managing the shift in only two trips. Now, as he got out of his car he heard the music blaring through the speakers into the stadium. Damn, he'd hoped they'd have finished by now. He strode along the corridors to his office and shut the door. He flicked on his computer and checked his email. Excellent, the test results he'd been waiting for had landed. He settled more comfortably in his chair and started to work through them. But his door was flung open less than ten minutes later.

'Gabe, good you're here, I need you to take a look at one of these girls.' Dion, the stadium CEO. Dion who had no problem watching the wannabe dancers auditioning.

'No.' Gabe didn't even glance up from his computer.

'Seriously, I need you. Bee sting. Looks like she's allergic.'

'Oh, you've got to be kidding. A bee sting?' Gabe growled. 'That would have to rank as the most pathetic attempt ever.'

'But genuine. You really—'

'Dion,' Gabe interrupted, still staring at his screen,

'I've seen sprained ankles, sore calves, strained wrists. All fake. But a bee sting is a first. Certainly more inventive…if it weren't for the fact that there are no bees on that pitch. They're banned from play with chemical spray.'

'Gabe—'

'Come on,' Gabe sighed with weary sarcasm. 'I don't want to deal with another desperate-to-date dancer. Enough, okay?'

More than enough. After causing a cold war in his family for a few years over his refusal to conform to tradition, and the horror of an ex-lover psycho stalking him, Gabe had learned a couple of things. Firstly, he wasn't limiting his life by getting married and therefore having to compromise on his own goals for the rest of his days. And to be sure of escaping that noose, he knew he had to make his intentions clear from the start, to only seek company from the equally sophisticated and never mess with a woman who had anything to do with his workplace. Especially this workplace where temptation, exacerbated by all the travel, was too much for most men anyway. He'd seen it so many times—embarrassingly short marriages, even more embarrassing scandals.

'I should have told you I'd brought her with me.' With a wicked grin Dion stepped further in and too late Gabe saw the smaller figure behind him. 'And for the record, I had to drag her here. She reckons she's fine but I don't agree.'

Oh, great. Gabe winced. The girl had to have heard every word. Still, that was probably good—dispelling any ideas she might have had. He pushed out from behind his desk and shot the departing Dion a foul look. Dion merely winked.

Gabe looked at his new patient. Her head was bent so

he couldn't see her face. Naturally she was blonde. And naturally the blonde wasn't natural at all. He could see the myriad colours streaked through the long length that fell in gentle curves past her shoulders. She had the long, slim limbs of the dancer. And the extremely brief attire. Then she looked up at him. Her eyes were red-rimmed but challenging. Her cheeks flushed. Her mouth full but firm. All instantly recognisable.

Good grief.

Gabe just stared, his brain fuzzy, a humming in his ears. He had to be mistaken on this. But he wasn't. This was his under-age *landlady*? Sleeping Beauty from the wilderness?

'Hello, Gabe.' Despite the colour in her cheeks, the rest of her face was deathly pale.

'What are you doing here?' he asked.

'You mean you haven't worked it out already?' Her wildly blue eyes glittered. But not from tears. No, it was all defiance.

His gaze narrowed. No, he couldn't believe *his* eyes. The mouse-brown hair was now shot through with gold. And there was so much polish. She was wearing marginally more than she had been yesterday. Actually the shorts were even shorter—micro shorts, the exact colour of her eyes. And instead of a see-through old vest-top, she had a pink leotard on. The whole outfit too skin-clinging for comfort.

'I thought you said you were going overseas,' he said stupidly.

'I am.' She looked at him through lashes perfectly—but heavily—mascaraed.

'Then why are you trying out for the Blades?' He swallowed. Was this high-gloss vision truly the same sodden waif he'd met less than twenty-four hours be-

fore? Helplessly he glanced down her leotard-clad torso
again. Not the slim waif at all. Curves had mushroomed
magically. He bit his lip to stop the smile and the comment he so badly wanted to make.

'I'm going overseas at the end of the season,' she said.
'I want to dance first.'

'The end of the season?' He was appalled; his amusement fled. That wasn't *soon*. He'd thought she was ship-
ping out in a week or so. How was he supposed to live
in that house with her a stone's throw away for the best
part of six months? Especially if she was going to be
glammed up something gorgeous like this?

'Yeah, except that stupid bee just ruined my chances.
And, no, I didn't stab myself with it just so I could get
your face up close to my inner thigh.'

Oh, my. Gabe snapped his mouth shut, worked hard
to bite back both the smile and the chuckle. His landlady had more fire than he'd given her credit for. He
walked closer, watched even closer. Her transformation
was something else, but he saw the hint of uncertainty in
her expression as he deliberately breached her personal
space. The girl was acting the grown-up. But some kind
of madness raced in his blood when she lifted her chin
and refused to break eye contact with him. Her audacious grit got to him. If she wanted to sharpen her kit-
ten claws, well, hell, he'd play up to her—a *very* little.
Frankly he couldn't resist seeing how far she'd go until
she melted in a flush, until she got tongue-tied and lost
her cool completely. He suspected it wouldn't be too far
at all.

'Do some of the dancers really fake injuries to come
and see you?' she asked outright.

Her obvious disbelief threw him instead. He cleared
his throat, knew he'd sounded like the most arrogant a-

hole ever. 'It's happened a couple of times.' More than a couple. But still.

Roxie giggled, suddenly delighted as she saw her tenant steal another quick look at her outfit—at least she'd achieved one objective today. Maybe it was the bee poison running through her system, or she was intoxicated by his proximity, but she couldn't resist baiting him—his arrogance was incredible. 'But you're not a rugby star. Surely the dancers have bigger fish to fry in this place? You know, all those *fit* young rugby players?'

He met her gaze with his dark one and a spark flickered in the depths. 'Maybe some of them prefer my qualifications.'

Heart racing, she breathed carefully to keep her answer cool. 'I'm sure more prefer the status and short-term income of the real stars.'

His smile was all shark. 'Maybe I have some other factors in my favour too.'

She figured he meant his looks. Yeah, so good-looking her toes were curling. All kinds of muscles clamped down—mostly in her nether regions. As if they were trying to dampen the inferno blazing there. 'Well, you don't need to worry about me, you're not my type,' she lied, feeling sassy and amused and surprisingly in control.

'No?'

She froze. She hadn't expected that direct challenge—his tone as loaded with tease as hers had been. She narrowed her gaze. 'Definitely not. You're too arrogant.'

Way too arrogant.

He leaned closer, his smile even more wicked. 'Lots of girls like arrogance. Confidence.'

'Lots of girls like bad boys too. I'm not like lots of girls.'

'That's true.' All of a sudden he frowned. 'Roxanna, *what* are you doing here?'

'Auditioning,' she cooed, to maintain the tease. 'And it's Roxie.'

Yeah, it was fun flexing flirt muscles that had been dormant so long. Really, it was easy. Because she could see the reaction—the glint in his eyes. And she could feel that pull between them; it was out-of-this-world strong.

'You told me Roxanna yesterday.' He stepped that little bit closer, his voice dropping.

'You caught me by surprise yesterday,' she breathed softly, holding eye contact. Nerves squeezed down tighter in her lower belly.

His gaze travelled across her face—eyes, lips, then dipped to her chest. 'So now you're Roxie.'

'Yes.' She tossed her hair defiantly and lifted her chin at him. 'I've always been Roxie.' Inside she had anyway. And 'Roxie' was certainly having an effect on him. She wasn't a total innocent. She'd had a boyfriend—one who had let her down in her hour of need, for sure, but she knew the look—and there was no disguising the look Gabe was giving her now. Oh, it had been worth every cent, every never-ending minute in the salon this morning. Poor Roxanna had never stood a chance, but add a little blonde, a little oomph to her assets? It was a different story. She couldn't believe men could be so shallow. But right now she didn't care, she was just basking in the heat in those eyes. The novelty was heady.

He shook his head very slowly. 'Well, Roxie, we'd better take a look at it.'

Look at what? Oh, her bee sting. She looked down at it and sighed; seemed as if the fun moment was over.

'I want you on the bed.'

Roxie almost gasped at that instruction, until she

quickly looked up and caught his too-bland expression. He was baiting her right back.

But he frowned when he glimpsed the circle of red, swollen skin on the inside of her thigh when she moved and sat up on the narrow bed against the wall. 'You weren't kidding.'

'Of course not,' she grumbled. As if she'd make up a bee sting just to get within cooee of the team doctor. He had such an inflated opinion of himself. 'Hurts like hell.'

He bent to look more closely. 'You can see the mark, but it looks like the actual sting is out. You've always been allergic?'

She nodded. 'But I haven't been stung in years. I thought I might have outgrown it.'

'Shame,' he murmured with evil intent, his breath a warm cloud brushing her thigh. 'When you've gone to such effort to grow up in other ways.'

She felt a very un-grown-up urge to throw something at him and his patronising attitude.

'Never mind, Roxie.' His bedside manner came out more like a taunt. 'Maybe you'll get to dance overseas.'

'Maybe.' She shrugged like as if she didn't mind, as if it wasn't the disappointment of the year.

'Spread your legs wider,' he instructed casually, but with that dangerous glint back in his eye.

Externally she froze, internally she melted. 'How wide?' she managed to ask.

'Wide enough for me, of course.' His expression was now pure challenge, purely expectant of...*what*?

She saw the barely suppressed smirk. He was amusing himself at her expense? Well, two could play at that game. Roxie determinedly imagined diving into Antarctic waters, cool—*freezing*—waters. Anything to keep her blush at bay. She was not going to go all girly embarrassed here, even though she felt it. Instead, she leaned back on her hands, tossed her head so her hair flicked out of her eyes. And she—who'd never spread her legs for any man—spread them as wide as they'd go. Which, given she could do the splits three ways, was actually quite wide. 'This okay?' she asked huskily.

He looked. Down then back up. Opened his mouth. Closed it. Swallowed as he looked down again. 'Just about,' he murmured and stepped right into place—mere inches separating them.

She ignored the flush she knew just had to be covering every inch of her skin and smiled the smile of total success. 'I didn't know you promised to flirt with your patients when you took the Hippocratic oath.'

'You're not a patient.' His gaze snapped up to her face.

'No? Aren't you tending to me, Mr Physician?'

'No. Not as a medical professional. I'm just going to hand you some cream and you can rub it on that sting yourself.'

She didn't know what had come over her, but the need to tease more was impossible to ignore. For the first time in her life she was flooded with confidence. She could say anything and not give a damn—the more provocative, the better, because his rapid response—desire mixed with defence—fuelled her wicked excitement. 'You're not going to rub it on for me?' she purred.

'No.' He stepped back. 'I am not.'

'Oh.' She looked down innocently. 'Do you only like rubbing cream on those big rugby boys?'

'Roxie.' He came back close, too close, his expression goaded. He studied her silently, ensuring he had her attention, then deliberately looked down her body in a blatantly sexual appraisal. 'Your hair isn't the only thing about you that's changed.'

He was looking at her chest. And, yes, he knew the truth for sure.

She lifted her chin, refusing to let embarrassment rise. 'It's amazing what supportive underwear can do for a girl.'

'Quite amazing,' he agreed drily. Suddenly he chuckled, that wholly amused sound that stirred that instinctive response in her to draw closer—and the temptation to tease further.

Yeah, she couldn't help but giggle back, despite the tension that still threaded through her. If anything the shared amusement pulled that thread tighter. 'You don't think my rack's real?'

'We both know it's not.'

Yeah, they did both know that. She angled her head down but peeped back up at him, batting her lashes to totally ham it up. 'But you have to admit, if you didn't know better, you'd be completely fooled.'

He took a moment to study her again, slow, deliberate consideration. 'Completely.'

She decided to push for more. 'And even though you know the truth, you like the effect anyway?'

The deep breath he drew in seemed to be painful, because he grimaced at the same time. Then he shook his head. 'It's false advertising. What happens if you pull one of those rugby boys—how you going to cope when he finds out the truth? Or are you going to offer to cook the chicken fillets for supper after?'

She wrinkled her nose but appreciated the attempt to shoot her down. 'Not chicken fillets. They'd stink something awful.'

'What's in there, then, cotton wool?'

'Gel pads. Much more comfortable. Natural feeling.'

'They feel natural?'

She shot a look into the deep, dark eyes that were only a few inches from her own. 'You want to find out for yourself?'

Oh, the challenge was out now. She could see him thinking, deciding…

'Roxie…' He cleared his throat and turned away quickly, went to a cupboard and pushed packets around in it with fierce concentration.

Disappointment burst her fantasy bubble. She looked down at her leg, suddenly the pain that had been muted screamed. She saw how the red was spreading, the swelling thickening.

'The reaction is getting worse,' she muttered, biting her lip because her thigh was hot, itchy and sore.

'It certainly is,' he answered abruptly, returning from the cupboard, still not looking at her directly. He pierced the seal on the small tube, squeezed some of the white cream onto the tips of his fingers. 'I'll give you a couple of antihistamine tablets as well. Have them when you get home—they might make you drowsy.'

She nodded, not able to speak any more. He'd gently spread her legs wider again and with fingers was smoothing the cream across the hot, tight skin. Seemed he'd forgotten he was going to make her do that herself. She looked at him as he watched what he was doing. Now she knew exactly why all those dancers faked injuries to get him to tend them—he was fun. And he truly was gorgeous with his perfect features and height. So very male. So very close. Touching her in a way that suggested other kinds of touch might be even more moving. Her lashes lowered as the tips of his fingers circled carefully, narrowing in on the sting site. She shouldn't be feeling it so sensually, but she was. She shouldn't be imagining those fingers gliding higher, but she was. She shouldn't be heating, melting, wanting—but she was. And she couldn't help the small shudder as he stroked in that smooth, regular rhythm.

He looked up; his eyes bored into hers. All tease gone and nothing but banked fire in the black eyes. 'You need to do this yourself.' Honest, raw—faint sheen sparkled on his skin as if he too felt a fever.

Her throat tightened, rendering her mute. So she nodded. But even that took effort. It was as if he'd some spell cast over her. Her heart wasn't racing, it was thumping so slowly, and every beat was so huge it hurt. She thought her eardrums were going to burst with the pressure. Both his hands rested on her now, no longer rubbing the cream, but holding her thigh. He could tighten his grip any moment.

If he wanted.

His gaze dropped a couple of inches south of her eyes. She knew what he was thinking about. She was thinking about it too. Wanted it. Her lips tingled, dried, she was desperately trying not to lick them. Suddenly he was closer, so close that—

'Hey, Gabe, how's our new girl?'

Gabe moved so fast Roxie didn't have time to blink before he was at the sink, running taps and scrubbing his hands.

'You mean me?' Roxie stared at the vivacious blonder than blonde who'd just burst into the room. Chelsea, the leader of the dance troupe.

'Yeah, are you okay?' Chelsea came up close to look at Roxie's leg. 'Looks ouch.'

'It's okay.' Seriously, she'd forgotten it in that over-

powering moment with his hands on her. 'Really, I'm…
just fine.' Just breathless.

'Great. Because up to the bee thing, you blew us away.
We want you in.'

'You do?' Roxie gaped. 'Really?' She'd thought she'd
blown it with the whole allergic-reaction-and-screams-
of-agony routine.

'Yeah, you're classically trained, right?'

'It was obvious?' She was stunned; she hadn't been
to a ballet class since she was sixteen.

'Not in a bad way, but I thought I could spot that un-
derlying technique a couple of times. Your freestyle was
amazing and I totally want to raid your moves. I've not
seen a girl break the way you do. We need some edge
and you definitely have it.'

Wow. No one had ever said she had 'edge' before.
Then again, no one had seen her dance in years. She'd
gone into that all but empty stadium today and just given
it everything. And she'd done it.

Elation added to the excitement that had already been
flooding her. She couldn't resist glancing at the tall, dark
torment now standing a few paces behind Chelsea. But
in the split second she looked, she saw the naked emotion on his face.

Anger.

His thunderous expression momentarily crushed her
mood. Why did he look so *bothered*?

'I'll leave these pills for you here.' He brushed past
Chelsea and brusquely put a small pill pack on the edge
of the table. He left the room faster than a streaker ran
the length of the pitch in an international match.

'Hottest thing on two legs, isn't he?' said Chelsea a
few seconds after he'd shut the door one decibel short
of a slam.

'I'm sorry?' Roxie blinked, still absorbing his massive mood swing.

'Gabe,' Chelsea explained. 'Hotter than any of those players. Fit plus brains plus wads of old money.'

'Really?' Roxie hoped her suddenly ravenous curiosity wasn't too obvious.

'Yeah but don't bother looking. See how he shot out of here the second he could?'

Roxie just nodded.

Chelsea sighed almost sadly. 'He used to be so outrageous, dated a different woman every night. Absolute slayer.'

Roxie carefully picked up the tube of cream he'd left on the narrow bed beside her and concentrated extra hard on screwing the cap back on. 'What changed that?'

'His ex Diana went crazy for him. Literally crazy.' Chelsea stepped nearer, her bubbly voice dropping conspiratorially. 'She was a dancer here, they didn't even date all that long but she tried to move in on him. I mean, she really did move in one weekend when he was away. It almost got to restraining-order point, but she had a breakdown and her family got her some help.' Chelsea looked awkward about sharing the info, but she talked on anyway. 'It wasn't his fault, she was delusional. Everyone knows he's never going to put one of these on a girl's finger.' Chelsea waggled the fingers of her left hand, and the flash of her massive diamond engagement ring temporarily blinded Roxie. 'Gabe's a playboy to the grave. Or he was. Now he's a repressed playboy.' Chelsea frowned and fixed Roxie in place with a searching look. 'When he smiles—too rare these days—all females instantly melt. There's not a woman in the world who wouldn't fancy him.'

Roxie knew denial would be too revealing and Chelsea

was looking as if she could see straight through her anyway. 'Well, he is very attractive.'

'Yeah, but he's unattainable,' Chelsea warned. 'Which makes him all the more attractive to so many women.' She half laughed and then instantly sobered. 'But don't waste your time. He's signed off from the game. Look, I've been with my man so long the others call me matron, but I still know how it works in this place—you get a bunch of fit guys together with a bunch of fit girls and it's all going to happen. There are twenty-odd gorgeous young things on that team who'd love to play. So if you want, go for it with one of them, just be sure to play safe.'

Roxie swallowed and stood up from the bed, letting her hair fall forward so the blush in her cheeks wouldn't be so obvious. Now probably wasn't the time to admit she'd never played at all—well, not all the way through a game. And she hadn't looked twice at any of the players—but their doctor? She stepped to get the pills so Chelsea couldn't see her face as she asked, 'Why did that girl go so crazy for Gabe?'

'You've got eyes, right?'

'Yeah, but sometimes good-lookers don't think they have to make any effort.' She'd read that in a magazine. She turned to get Chelsea's answer.

'Rumour has it his technique is even better than his body. I don't know the truth of that myself but I'd believe it.' Chelsea looked worried. 'Look, so many girls have tried it with him and failed in the last few months since Diana. Save yourself the humiliation—I've seen them fall but he rejects *harshly* and then they resign. I don't want to lose another dancer, especially one as interesting as you, so *please* don't go after him.'

Roxie laughed—she'd never gone after a guy in her

life; she wouldn't know where to start. 'Don't worry, I won't.'

And she didn't want to jeopardise her spot on the Blades—she'd wanted that for too long. But a part deep inside her flamed because Gabe had *wanted* to kiss her. She might not be all that experienced but she'd known that. Which meant he wasn't entirely unattainable. Oh, yes, temptation whispered—tantalising her with the fantasy. She wanted that experience—to finally take a lover and a damn good one. If Gabe was that great, couldn't he be the one to do it all with? Clearly he didn't want commitment—none of that lovelorn, clinging stuff. But nor did she. She had no intention of being pulled into a relationship. Her freedom had been a long time in coming and she wasn't giving it up for anyone.

Hours later, as he drove to his new home Gabe rationalised. It didn't matter, the Blades only rehearsed on site once a week and he was well used to avoiding them at that time anyway. She'd be there during the games, but he was busy with the boys for all that time. He didn't attend the after-match functions at the home stadium as a rule now. So while he might glimpse her every now and then, that would be it. He could live with that for just this season. Sure he could.

But when he got to the Treehouse he couldn't help looking at the window above the garage. The curtain wasn't drawn; there was no sign of life. The garage was locked but a wall of boxes blocked the back window so he couldn't see if a car was parked in there. He had no way of knowing whether she was home or not. Unless he knocked on her door.

The tablets he'd given her could cause drowsiness. He sighed. So what? That was no reason to bother. She'd be fine. Only there were probably druggies and vagrants in that park in the dark of the night. And she was on the edge of it, alone. In a room above a rickety garage that had to be the size of a postage stamp. Yeah, the niggle turned into a nag and then into a frankly disturbing level of worry. The only way to get rid of it was to see her for himself and thus be sure she was okay. And that was the only reason he wanted to see her. Medical—a professional capacity. But he wasn't her doctor or anything. He was determined *not* to be that. A concerned acquaintance?

Oh, bugger it. He thumped up the stairs, hoping to make enough noise to ensure she'd hear his arrival. He rapped hard on the door. Rapped harder. Shouted out her name. It was at the point when he was considering smashing the lock that he heard a grumbling response.

Finally the door swung open.

At first all he saw was the tee shirt. Less than a second later realised that all she wore was the tee shirt. Cute, cotton, white thing. Maybe there were knickers, but maybe not. His tongue gummed to the roof of his mouth.

'Is everything okay?' Drowsily she tucked her hair back behind her ears.

'That's what I was coming to ask you,' he muttered, barely more intelligible than a grunting Neanderthal. Even sleepy her eyes sparkled. He then made the massive mistake of glancing down. Thighs, calves, ankles. Her long, tanned legs that were slender but also hinted at strength. Yeah, supple muscles were shown off under the gorgeous stretch of golden skin and he wanted to reach out and run his fingers down their warm length. Wanted them to spread again for him.

'I think it's okay,' she said huskily. 'It doesn't seem to be any worse.'

He flinched. He'd totally forgotten about the sting, he'd just been checking her out and wondering about the undies. And now she held her leg slightly outstretched meaning he caught the glimpse of lace-edged silk covering her crotch. His tongue actually tingled as the urge to drop to his knees hit him. He wanted to lick her there. Oh, hell, everywhere.

Cotton tee shirt. He frowned, forced himself to think on the cotton. Not the lace knickers. Sweet not sexy. Not sophisticated. Not appropriate. She was his landlady. This would be mess-up central if he followed the path his body was determinedly dragging him towards. He swallowed, furious with his rapid descent into peeping Tom territory. 'Make sure you reapply the cream.' He snapped more than he meant to.

Her sleepy blue eyes widened. 'Why are you so grumpy?'

He glowered. 'I'm not.'

'Oh, you so are.' She grinned, undaunted. 'But I think it's still there, buried beneath the frown.'

'What's still there?' He couldn't resist asking.

'The ability to have fun.'

The tiny tot was back at flirting? 'Oh, I have fun,' he said deliberately slowly. 'But I'm selective about who I have fun with.'

'That's very wise.' She nodded guilelessly. 'I'm very selective myself.'

Oh, really? His muscles sharpened. 'How much fun have you had?'

Her lashes drooped; she almost pouted. 'Not enough.'

He determinedly looked past her so he wouldn't be tempted to touch those full lips. 'Looks like you've been having a bit.' He nodded towards the empty bottle in the middle of the dining table.

She turned to see what he meant. 'Oh, that…' she swung back, her smile impish '…was good.'

He took the opportunity of her movement to step past her into the room. And was dead unimpressed with what he could see. Furniture from one corner to the other. Furniture on top of furniture, boxes above and below. A tiny single stretcher crammed under the window was her bed? He winced at its obvious discomfort—hard and definitely too short for him. How could she stand it?

'You can't be serious about living here,' he said, all grump again.

'Why not?' she answered coldly.

'There's no *room*.' There wasn't an inch of spare floor space. A half metre square in which to get in from the door and then, bam, *stuff.*

'There's more than enough room for me.'

He looked down at her—too close—in the too small space. Quickly he looked back to the table, anything to stop himself taking rampant advantage of the lack of space. He noticed an 'H' written in permanent marker in the top corner of the wine label. 'What's the H for?'

She glanced at the table and her expression turned guilty.

Why? 'Got any more?' he couldn't help teasing.

He glanced round; behind him was a fridge. He shot her a look and reached out a hand. It was literally a bar fridge—and, yes, filled with alcohol. He hadn't actually expected that. The only other item was an oversized container of hummus. 'How many bottles you got in here?' He held the door open, amazed.

'Five,' she said defensively. 'And they're only half bottles.'

He drew one out, saw the single capital letter on the label, bent and saw they each had different letters. 'What do they stand for?'

Roxie folded her arms, never going to admit that she'd blown his rent advance on getting her hair done, some new underwear and half a dozen half-bottles of champagne. 'None of your business.'

'No, go on, they obviously mean something.' Relentlessly he waited.

'All right, H was for getting my hair done.' She defiantly ran her fingers through her hair, flicking it so it fell over her shoulder, almost long enough to cover her breast. Almost. 'I'd waited ages for that.' And she'd drunk it early—to celebrate getting her tenant and the money *for* the haircut. She watched him drag his gaze from the ends of her hair back to the bottles in the fridge.

'What about the P?' he asked.

'For my first public performance.' She stepped forward, quickly trying to explain them all so he'd leave. Trying to think up something for the one whose purpose was flashing neon-sign style in her head. 'T is for when I book my ticket overseas. D is for when I get my driver's licence.' She winced when she said that one—now he'd really think she was a kid. 'A was for the audition—getting through to the Blades. I'm going to have it later.'

'Who are you going to have it with?' he asked.

You? Roxie slammed her mouth shut on the instant-response answer and took a half-second to come up with something sassier. 'It's only a half-bottle. I'm going to have it all by myself.'

His brows lifted. 'Did you have the first all by yourself?'

'Absolutely.' She smiled, pleased with her ability to keep talking in the face of his gorgeousness.

'Didn't it have a bit of a kick?'

'Fantastic.' She nodded.

He finally grinned back. 'No headache?'

'That's why I got the good stuff.' And she was feeling far more of a kick from the way he was smiling. She was positively giddy and she certainly hadn't been giddy from the champagne last night.

'Have enough of it and you'll still get a hangover.' He actually laughed then. 'You should share them with someone.' His voice dropped.

'Never,' she dismissed him instantly. Dismissing the outrageous invite on the tip of her tongue too. 'Do you know the price of each one of those bottles? It's mine, all mine.'

He chuckled and looked back at the fridge. 'And V, what's that one for?'

Damn, she'd hoped he might have forgotten about that last one. She swallowed, wished her addled brain would come up with something—anything to get her out of this embarrassment.

'Victory?' he asked.

'Yeah.' She nodded enthusiastically. So not going to admit to this guy that the last bottle of Bollinger was for when she finally lost the virginity she'd been dragging round for far too long. 'For when the Knights win the trophy.'

'You drink champagne all the time?'

Uh, try never before last night. 'On special occasions.'

He closed the fridge and eyed her, looking serious now. 'Mind if I ask you a personal question?'

'Go right ahead.' She waited, wondered.

'How old are you?'

She hadn't expected that. 'Twenty-two.'

His mouth thinned.

'That surprises you?' *Unpleasantly?* Why was he looking so unimpressed?

'I thought you were younger.' He swallowed.

Uh-huh. 'How young?'

'Eighteen or so.'

At the most, she reckoned. What was with the putting her in a child's box? 'Well, how old are you?'

'Thirty-one.'

'There's less than a decade between us,' she pointed out with extreme pleasure.

'I'm still a lot older than you.' He seemed determined to labour that one.

'Yeah, but you're hardly old enough to be my father. Unless, of course, you were *very* advanced for your age,' she taunted softy, pleased to see him wince in horror.

'I was very advanced for my age in some areas,' he said, quickly reverting back to his blunt arrogance. 'But, no, I was nice and normal and didn't start fooling around 'til my teens.'

She gritted her teeth. A nice, *normal* teen life. She hadn't had that. She didn't resent the reasons why she hadn't, she had loved caring for her grandparents, but it was time now for her to have the freedom and fun she'd missed out on as an eighteen-year-old. Not to mention the fooling around. Better late than never and she was damn well determined it wouldn't be never. Maybe it could be soon. 'Well, as you now know, I'm more than old enough to be living on my own, in any way I like, drinking whatever I want.' And she'd do whatever she wanted too.

There was a moment's silence. He glanced at the fridge again. 'Do you eat anything?'

She knew he'd noticed the lack of oven. But there was the microwave and a single gas ring. Okay, she was pretty much camping. But it wasn't for ever and it was worth it. 'I usually make a salad or something.'

'From the garden big enough to feed a small island nation?' He turned away, his smile twisting. 'Well, make sure you eat a load tonight and don't have the champagne, given you've had those pills.'

She followed him to the door and leaned against the jamb, well aware that as she lifted her hand her tee shirt rose higher. Sure enough, she saw his eyes dart down. Her thighs burned, not because of the bee. She brushed her hair back from her face with her other hand and watched his gaze flicker first to her hair, then to her chest where her tee shirt had tightened across her bra-less breasts. Emboldened she answered him softly, full of feminine taunt. 'Gabe, I thought we'd just established that I'm not a child.'

His gaze shot to her eyes, intensified—the black pupils expanding to obliterate any hint of the molten colour. The muscles in his jaw were delineated as he clamped his mouth shut. Then he suddenly drew breath. 'You might not be a child, Roxie, but you are a bit too much of a babe for comfort.'

Roxie froze, her body so hot she was on the brink of incineration.

His gaze swept over her one last time before he turned away. 'So I think it's best we steer clear of each other.'

She watched him take the stairs three at a time as if he was escaping some terrible threat. She went back into her studio and smiled. In so many ways Gabe Hollingsworth was a challenge. And Roxie, for all her inexperience, had never backed down from a challenge.

Not even the most impossible.

CHAPTER THREE

GABE pounded round the park. If his apartment hadn't been leased already he'd have moved back into it. Because finding out her age had not helped. She had that extra five years he'd thought she'd get overseas. She had enough sophistication to tempt him to tease. But it was still wrong—with the landlady thing and the dancer thing.

But then there was the water torture. Every damn morning.

After the first night he'd slept at the Treehouse, he'd been woken by the gentle sound of running water. He'd peered out of the window, then *stared* out of the window. His eyes wide, his wayward cock gaining width too. Yeah, at five o'clock in the freaking morning he'd found out who the gardener was. And how well she danced. Now every morning he was literally *roused* by Roxie watering the garden, doing some kind of insane yogic stretching while the tomatoes got their drink. She warmed up her barely covered body while watering the damn plants. A music player clipped to her hip, headphones in her ears, her whole body swaying. It was enough to drive any man to drink straight spirits. By the gallon. From the way she moved—too sensually— he suspected she knew he watched. Of course he bloody

watched—what man wouldn't? And her deliberate prov-
ocation was working—despite his attempt to defuse it
between them and tell her keeping some distance was
best.

Yeah, he was dying of lust. Not only did she disturb
his dreams, but conscious moments when he didn't have
a tight leash on his imagination. He *ached*, hungry every
damn minute of the day.

So now, every morning, Gabe escaped by running
round the park, supposedly sticking well out of temptation's way. Only today, a week after he'd moved in, he
ran faster and harder than ever. No time at all before he
was back at the hidden gate and the giant padlock. And
behind that fence, watering the vegetables, Roxie was
bent over in those short, short shorts. He could see the
headphones in her ears as she bopped round the place,
thinking she was completely alone.

Yeah, okay, he'd known she'd still be there.

Breathing hard—and not because of the forty-minute
run he'd just been on—he walked closer and watched
her legs in action. Thanks to the headphones she had no
idea he was there. It was dangerous. Anyone could sneak
up on her. Anyone who saw the way she danced in her
backyard would be all over her. She needed to be taught
a lesson—that the headphones had to go, the shorts had
to be longer, the dancing needed to stay indoors.

He walked behind her, not bothering to be quiet, because he could hear the thumping beat of her music from
here. In a sudden movement he wrapped his arms around
her. He'd anticipated she'd jump, so he tightened his arms
so she couldn't flee. The hose did a snake dance on the
ground spraying them both, until he kicked it away with
his foot. The cold burst of water didn't cool his insanity
at all.

He let her twist round, feeling her fury, feeling his own fire as her breasts were brought flush against him. He almost growled with the satisfaction of finally having her this close.

'What are you doing?' she shrieked at him.

He plucked buds from her ears. 'No need to shout, I'm right here.'

'Well, why are you right here, sneaking up on me like this,' she panted.

It was sick how much he liked feeling her breathing hard against him. How hard he was breathing too. Oh, her eyes were blue this morning. And her hair in that loose plait with those recently shorn, blonder bits wisping round her face…

'Teaching you a lesson,' he muttered, putting both arms securely around her again. Tightening them.

'What lesson's that?' She looked stunned.

'That when you're alone in the garden, watering whatever and doing your workout, that anyone could sneak up on you.'

'Only some sicko.'

Yeah, like him. 'That's right. So you need to be more careful.'

Roxie was caught between fury and desire. In the first instance, fury won. She brought her knee up between his legs fast. Only slowing at the last possible second.

His eyes widened and he jerked—too late—she just brushed his balls.

'I could have got you really badly then,' she said severely.

He nodded. 'Thanks for not. I've never wanted kids but retaining the physical ability to have the option would be good.' He repositioned himself out of harm's way, but still didn't release her. 'But what if I'd had a weapon?'

'What exactly are you trying to do?' she confronted him. 'You're telling me I can't feel safe in my own backyard? What kind of a kick-in-the-teeth lesson is that?'

'I didn't mean that.' He suddenly frowned. 'I just think you should be careful.'

'I am careful, Gabe. And you know what? In the entire year that I've been living here alone, not one person has bothered to break in.'

No one had bothered to visit either. Honestly? No one had in years.

The silence lengthened. She was vaguely conscious of her rapid breathing, of his, of how close they were pressed together. But the main thing sucking all her attention was that deepening emotion in his eyes. She didn't know what it meant.

'I did,' he eventually said. 'I wanted to.'

Roxie just didn't know what to make of that. Her breathing deepened—so did his, until they were inhaling in sync. It finally occurred to her that she was staring. But she couldn't stop. Randomly she realised he'd been out running. She hadn't known he did that. She also had her palms wide on his shoulders. She wasn't moving them away. The warm, solid strength was wonderful. And arousing.

'You train every morning?' she asked softly, not wanting him to move either.

He nodded his head. 'I find it difficult to sleep in. Here.'

'Does my doing the garden bother you?'

'Yes.'

'Oh.' Too bad. She wasn't going to stop.

'You've always done it?' he asked quietly, inching even closer.

She nodded slowly.

'That's why you have the tan, why you're fit.' Oh, his voice was mesmerising, he was *all* mesmerising.

'That and the dancing.' She relaxed against him a fraction. Felt his tension increase.

'The dancing,' he repeated in a low mutter. 'Yeah.'

'I wear the headphones because I don't want to disturb the neighbours.' She looked up at him with eyes that hadn't blinked in so long they ached.

'You disturb the neighbours anyway. *This* neighbour.'

At her waist, his grip tightened. Then his fingers moved—pushing, creating a space between her tee shirt and waistband—accessing bare skin. She shuddered—an uncontrollable spasm of pleasure as one anticipation was fulfilled. More rose fast. Oh, this was good. This was very, very good.

'This is bad.' He seemed to be talking exclusively to her lips. 'This isn't happening.'

'Why not?' She slid her tongue across her excessively dry lower lip.

He tensed more. 'I'm not in the market for a relationship.'

'Nor am I,' she assured him.

He was silent.

But with his grip this firm on her, his gaze this firm, she grew bold. 'But I do want you...'

He remained silent, but the heat in his expression flared.

'To do me a favour,' she expanded, her voice even softer.

'What?' His gaze remained glued to her mouth.

She didn't know if he was really listening—but she was about to find out. 'Sleep with me.'

His focus shot to meet hers. She lifted her chin a notch, not retreating from her challenge.

His lips twisted. 'Have you had champagne for breakfast?'

She wished she had—it might make this easier. She repeated her new mantra. She was a free spirit, floating through life now. Unafraid to do what she wanted. And she'd take neither acceptance nor rejection to heart. 'I want you to be my lover.' She drew her lip in with her teeth and breathed the last. 'My first.'

His eyes widened. 'What?'

She waited, knowing full well he'd heard.

His hands gently shook her. 'Your *first*?'

A different kind of tension rolled off him now.

Okay, so maybe mentioning the 'first' had been a mistake. But she'd wanted him to know. Thought it was better to be honest. Thought it might tempt him all the more. Only a look of sheer panic scrunched his face. Now he dropped his hands and took a step back.

'Isn't it every man's fantasy?' she asked, suddenly a lot less confident.

'Not mine.'

'No?'

His jaw clamped for a moment; she saw the deep breath he dragged in. Then he lifted his chin. 'No. I don't want some total novice who doesn't know what she's doing. Who'll lie like a log expecting me to do all the work.'

Ouch. How to shoot her down. 'I'm not a total novice. The actual virginity bit is a mere technicality,' she flung at him, furious that he could go cold so quick—and be so damn brutal about it. Chelsea had been right about him being harsh; he had a really offensive kind of defence. But it was an act—she knew it. She'd felt the need in his body. 'I know you're interested,' she said defiantly. 'I've seen the way you look at me.'

'How do I look at you?'

'Like you want to touch.' She moved forward, her boldness returning when he didn't walk away. And damn it, she'd come this far, there was nothing left of her dignity to lose. So she wasn't just flirty, she was shameless. 'And I do know how to touch. Won't be any kind of cold stone.'

'Really?'

She nodded. Hoping her hammering nerves weren't obvious.

He stood like an immovable mountain. In fact she didn't see any part of him move as he murmured, 'Prove it.'

Part of her wanted to tell him to go to hell for playing her so hard. But victory surged through her veins too. Yes, she'd known. She might be a virgin but that didn't mean she was an idiot. He wanted her.

She got to within kissing distance. But she wasn't going to go for the obvious. Nor was she going to make it that easy for him. Somehow she was going to make him suffer for this humiliation.

She looked down his body—as freely, boldly, brazenly as he'd looked at her before. Then she stepped closer, angling her head so her face tucked in near his neck—her own neck exposed to him. She blew, very lightly, on the pulse she could see beating madly just beneath his jaw.

He flinched.

With one, light finger she stroked his forearm, feeling the heat of his skin, the tenseness of the muscles beneath it. She moved, licked her lips, then very lightly pressed them against his salty skin.

He stood like a statue. A very hot, breathing hard one.

'I have had a boyfriend. I know a few things,' she whispered against his throat. 'Done a few things.' Her hand moved to his chest, circling the tight nipple beneath his tee. 'And I'm keen to learn some more.'

She felt the rise and fall as his breathing quickened from just that little touch. And then he seemed to stop breathing altogether.

She moved her hips closer to his. Dancing just that little bit in front of him. Bringing her mouth closer to his throat again. She'd wanted to taste him for so long. She wrapped one arm around his lean waist, her other hand flat on his chest, fingers smoothing.

She felt his response. Rocked her hips closer to the thick erection but pulled back at the last millimetre— *almost* touching, *almost* thrusting against him. But not quite.

She snuck a very quick look at his face. His eyes were shut tight. The muscles in his jaw stood out. His fists clenched at his sides. She felt heady pleasure at seeing how she affected him. But she didn't want him to be in such rigid control. Her instinct was to soften more against him. To come closer, to drape like silk over him. But she sensed that this slightest of distances between them was doing her cause some good.

She rose on tiptoe and gently scraped his ear lobe with her teeth, then whispered, 'I won't just be lying there, Gabe.'

It would be impossible anyway. Her hips had a mind of their own, circling near him in that rhythm that was ancient and instinctive.

He moved, hands slamming her body against his. His fingers digging into her hips. His erection doing the same to her belly. He held her firm, clamping her to him so she couldn't move. Pressed together like this, with only the fabric separating them, she didn't want to. His hardness, her softness. She let her head fall back to meet his fiery gaze, her position wholly submissive as he took her weight. But her eyes and mouth teased.

'Why now?' he asked through tightly clamped teeth.

'It's a good time.' And that was the truth.

'Why me?'

'Isn't it obvious?' she asked breathily. 'Just as it's obvious you want me as much.'

'Only a gay man could fail to react to this stunt of yours,' he growled. 'Even then I reckon he'd rise to it. But that doesn't mean I'm going to follow through.'

Cold seeped into her skin, stiffening her. She straightened as she felt his physical withdrawal. 'Why not?'

'I'm flattered, Roxie.' He stepped back and let her go. 'But this isn't the right thing for you.'

Who was he to judge that? Only she knew what was right for her. 'I'm not a child.'

'No, but you are a lot less experienced than I am. I don't think you've thought this through.'

'Don't insult me.' She'd thought of nothing else for days. 'I've not been hanging onto my chastity for the one and only. It's been more circumstance than design.'

'What, you're an accidental virgin?' he said sarcastically.

'Yeah, for want of a better description, I guess I am.' Jake, her ex-boyfriend, hadn't understood her situation at all. Had run out of patience when she'd said she couldn't go clubbing or partying with him. Yeah, she'd learned years ago that people didn't want to hear about her life—that it made them uncomfortable. After he'd dumped her, she'd gotten so busy at home it was the last thing on her mind. But it was there now.

'That's what that other bottle of Bollinger is for, isn't it?' Gabe said slowly. 'The V bottle. Good grief. You can't be so premeditated about this.'

'Why not? Isn't it better to be prepared with someone suitable rather than have some impulsive experience with someone who might not be able to deliver.' She wanted a good lover and she *knew* Gabe would be more than good. Her physical reaction to him was so intense and an absolute first. She wanted to follow through on it—just knew it would be incredible.

'This isn't impulsive?' He ran both hands through his hair and then bent to pick up the hose and turned it on the garden.

'I thought you might appreciate my honesty. That was clearly a mistake.' She pushed out a deep breath, trying to expel her anger. 'I won't make that one again.'

'What do you mean?' He jerked back to face her.

'Next time I proposition a guy I won't mention the "v" word.'

His jaw dropped. 'Are you planning to proposition another guy?'

'Maybe not today, but hopefully soon,' she bluffed, wishing she could meet someone even more attractive first thing so she could get over the ache she had for the impossible one in front of her.

'You have to tell him you're a virgin,' Gabe snapped.

As if she'd ever do that now. 'Why? It shouldn't make any difference.'

'Of course it makes a difference,' he said, looking angrier than ever. 'You should want someone who's in love with you and who you're in love with.'

She gaped at him. Who'd have thought the supposed ultimate slayer had a romantic streak? 'Were you in love with your first?' she asked.

'That was different.' He turned back to the garden, spraying the hose wildly over the paths rather than the plants.

'Why? Because you're a man and it's different for men?' She glowered at him. 'Why can't I have sex just for the pleasure of it, for the curiosity. Why did you have sex that first time?'

He growled. 'It's not the same.'

'Why not?' Her voice rose. 'Why can't women have the same kind of sex drive? is it somehow wrong to admit to it?'

His knuckles were white on the hose. 'No, but don't throw it away on some skunk. It's a gift you should give someone who'll appreciate it.'

Roxie groaned in frustration, too cross to care about how indiscreet she was being. 'I never thought you'd be so old-fashioned. Your reputation is so wrong.'

He tossed the hose and grabbed her arm instead. His grip so hard his knuckles remained white. Not that she minded that much, truthfully—her skin sizzled from his touch, and her insides melted.

'Is that why you picked me?' he asked. 'Because of something you heard, something you think you know?'

His anger made her own flare again and she pushed even closer to his tense fury. 'I asked you because you're hot. And, yeah, rumour has it you're good and you're not interested in commitment. All three are on my essential list.'

'Most women have commitment-friendly on their essential list,' he snapped back, his black eyes incandescent. 'Why don't you?'

'Because I don't want to be tied down. *Ever.*'

His brief bark of laughter was filled with disbelief. 'So there's going to be no marriage, kids and people carrier for you?'

'Never.'

He grinned savagely but his grip on her eased. 'Never is a very long time for a young woman.'

'Don't patronise me.' Jerk. 'I know what I want and what I don't want.' She wasn't going through the heart-ache that family brought again. She just wasn't ever. She had the need-to-be-free gene and she wasn't going to screw it up as her mother had by having a child or any kind of lengthy relationship.

'What you want is someone who'll do right by you,' he said, harsh again.

'And you won't? You're saying you're not up to the challenge?' She leaned so close she nearly kissed him as she whispered in a low taunt, 'You're not good enough as a lover?'

'Don't try to tease me into it,' he said through gritted teeth, letting go of her completely. 'It won't work.'

'Won't it?' She looked down his body, brazen in her assessment of his aroused state. 'You're only human, Gabe.'

'That's right, I'm human. I'm not an animal. I have self-control and free will. Choice.' He drew in a deep breath and then pushed back her braid from her shoulder with a surprisingly gentle hand. 'Are you going to use your innocent wiles to try to tempt me into losing that control?'

Silent, she just looked at him. Because, hell, yes, she wished she could do just that. It would so totally serve him right.

A wicked, patronising grin made him look like a smug satyr. 'You think you can play with fire, Roxie?'

'You're the fire?' she scorned. 'You're so not the blaze I'd heard about. All you are is insufferably arrogant.'

'Well, haven't you just given me more reason to be?' he drawled back, before snapping, 'I'm doing what's best for both of us. And, honey, you're not hot enough for me.'

She knew what he was doing. Pushing her away by putting her down. Bastard. 'Making me mad with you isn't going to make me want you less,' she said brazenly. If anything it made it worse. Yeah, now she wanted to see him shaking with desire for her—on his damn *knees* for her. 'I'm more than hot enough for you. I might be a virgin but I'm not stupid.'

His grin died an instant death. 'And that's another reason to say no.' He walked further away that time. 'This conversation is over. We'll pretend it never happened. Landlord, tenant, vague acquaintance at the stadium. That's all we are.'

Roxie remained where she was, feet apart, skin burning, senses screaming to be back in touch zone. 'Let me remind you, Gabe, that you were the one who started this.'

Gabe stopped and turned, his body howling at him for doing this hatefully 'right' thing in such a rubbish way. Being chivalrous really wasn't all it was cracked up to be and it was almost impossible. But now there was no choice—no matter her age or intelligence, learning Roxie was that inexperienced ruled out any kind of thing between them. He refused to be the cause of another girl's emotional—and mental—meltdown. And he was an absolute fool for taunting her into touching him just then; it had brought nothing but more torture for himself. 'I think we could debate that one for some time too. But for now, okay, I'll take the blame. I'm not too filled with self-worth to be unable to admit I make mistakes. This was a huge mistake. We're not making it worse.'

Yeah, as if he could really think that. Honestly?

It couldn't get any worse.

CHAPTER FOUR

'SEEN the new dancer?' Dion asked him as they watched the boys doing their drills that afternoon. 'Your bee-sting girl got in and she's good.'

She wasn't his bee-sting girl. And he was trying very hard not to watch the women doing the warm-ups down the other end of the pitch. Usually they made it a rule not to practise when the girls were around—it was too distracting. But it was the day before the first big game of the season and everyone wanted extra pitch time.

'Foxy Roxie.' Dion's smile was pure evil.

Gabe nearly jumped out of his skin. 'Who's calling her that?' He consciously tried to relax but his body had been nuked and he was boiling from the inside out.

'Jimmy, couple of those new kids. Got their eyes trained.'

Foxy Roxie wasn't that at all. She might have her hair blonded and her eyelashes blackened and her breasts pushed up front and centre, but that was all surface. The suggestion of sophistication was merely skin deep. She was an innocent at large. Admittedly she didn't want to be innocent but that was beside the point. She still was. And he didn't want any of those louts taking advantage of her. No, truth was, he wanted to take total advantage himself.

'She's just a kid.' He tried to act dismissive and completely blanked Dion's snort of laughter.

Inevitably the two groups met up as practice ended. It was brief, management were watching close to make sure the boys didn't get up to bad the night before a big game. She stood on the edge of the circle of dancers, not saying anything, a little distanced. Probably because she was new. But it was only a matter of time before one of the guys would strike up a conversation with her. Sure enough, one of the young bloods took a buddy as back-up. Shook her hand and everything. But Roxie had a back-up too, another dancer who was doing all the talking while Roxie had a Mona Lisa smile on.

Gabe didn't like her standing that near to any of them. As he watched she flicked a glance at him. Her blue eyes burned brighter—and she smiled wider at the guy beside her. Gabe knew she was doing it deliberately to tease him. Because every few moments she glanced back at him, saw him watching and her blue eyes burned brighter.

So, yes, he was staring. And, no, he couldn't stop. The thought of her hooking up with someone else ate him whole.

When she went to put her empty electrolyte bottle in the recycling bin he took the chance to talk. 'Don't do anything dumb.'

He'd been a jerk to her—several times over—and he deeply regretted it. But he didn't want her making a worse mistake out of hurt pride. Of course, complete louse that he was, the thing he regretted most was not kissing her.

'Didn't think you cared,' she said with an annoying level of composure.

He hesitated.

She smiled, drawing his attention to her glossed lips. Yeah, he totally regretted not kissing her. It was all he'd been thinking about since—how soft and hot she'd been in his arms, how vibrant, how beautiful. Fresh as a damn daisy.

'You had your chance,' she said with a smugness that suggested she could read his mind.

'You'd go off with just anyone?' he asked snarkily.

'Not just anyone. I'm sizing them up. You know them well, got any recommendations for me?'

'Not funny.'

It really wasn't. But she chuckled anyway.

'Not one of those guys would be any good,' he said firmly. Would it be bad if he told her they all had STDs? Yeah, defamatory and enough to cost him his job.

'None as good as you, right?' Her eyes sparkled. 'Oh, Gabe, ever heard of the dog in the manger?'

'I just think you're making a mistake.' Massive mistake. And the idea of it was killing him.

'No, I'm getting on with my life. There are lots of things I want to do. This is just one of them.'

'Well, do some other things first.' He thought half desperately. 'Go swim with dolphins or something—wouldn't that be good?'

She put on a thoughtful pose and her eyes went bluer than that fantasy ocean he wanted her to dive into—alone. 'I guess that would be good. I'll add it to my list. But right now I'm enjoying flirting.'

He put his hand on her arm to stop her, couldn't resist that smallest touch. 'Some of these boys don't know how to do slow,' he warned.

She turned back to face him, her smile slaying all his good intentions. 'Who said anything about slow?'

She pulled her arm free and sauntered back to the

group of girls and their hangers on, and Gabe was left with his jaw hanging mid-air. Yeah, he couldn't leave. Just stood, ostensibly laughing at some of the jokes with the guys, but, really, watching her like a damn hawk and mad with himself for obsessing. It was only because he'd put her out of bounds that he wanted her so much, right?

The boys started to go, keen to get an early night. But those two talking to her were still here. Then she moved. So, naturally, Gabe did too.

'You're leaving?' He caught up to her as she headed towards the corridor.

'Yes, I'm leaving,' she confirmed sarcastically.

'Alone?' Oh, he was so enthralled he had to ask more to be sure. It was pathetic.

'Gabe, it's the night before the first big game of the season. You really think any of those boys are going to go for an up-all-nighter with me now?'

Actually he wouldn't blame any of those boys for picking pleasure with her over being sensible the night before the season starter. But it seemed they were more professional than he was. Had more self-control. He glanced back at the group of them and saw several watching her. Yeah, she was the new crush. He walked out with her, happy to let them see it. If they thought he had a claim, that was fine by him. He didn't give a damn about maintaining his no-dating-in-the-stadium distance this second.

He walked with her to the car park, watched when she stopped and pulled a key from her pocket. 'This is your car?'

Roxie paused—he was all wide-eyed and animated as he took in the gleaming metal—and she couldn't hold back her smile any more. 'Sure is.'

He blinked a couple of times before running a hand

over the bonnet. 'Wouldn't have expected that.' Only then he frowned. 'But doesn't one of your Bolly bottles have D on it? For *driver's*…' His gaze narrowed and he whirled towards her. 'Show me your licence.'

'Only when you show me your badge, *officer*,' she drawled, finding such pleasure in mocking him. She was in way too good a mood because he hadn't wanted her to flirt with those others. That in fact he'd followed her out and hadn't seemed to care that everyone had watched him do it.

'You're driving illegally.' He looked amazed and suddenly laughed. 'I can't believe that Miss Goody Two-Shoes is driving illegally.'

She steeled herself to resist her melt reaction to his laughter. 'Why do you think I'm Miss Goody Two-Shoes?'

'Oh, come on.' He met her gaze with that warm humour glinting in his own. 'You're totally good. You *told* me how good.'

She sighed and exaggeratedly rolled her eyes. 'I really don't think virginity ought to have anything to do with whether a girl is "good" or not. You need to get over your outdated stereotypes of women.'

His grin went totally wicked. 'You're right. But you dare take me to task about stereotypes? What about your new hairdo, your fake breasts, your sudden decision to shimmy and shake it all in public? Truth is you live in a hideout and garden instead of partying. You're Roxanna not Foxy Roxie, you're playing at being a sophisticated vamp go-go dancer. Question is why?'

Foxy Roxie? Oh, she wished. 'I'm not playing at anything. What do you think I am, some toddler who's got into her mother's make-up drawer? So you saw me before I had my hair done, so what? I'm capable of more bad than you can ever imagine.' And she was thinking *such* bad thoughts this second. And just because she'd never acted on them much in the past, didn't mean she wouldn't in the future—or *now*.

The glint of humour got lost in the brilliant blackness of his eyes. 'Actually I can imagine.' His voice dropped. 'Believe me, I can.'

She turned her back on him and his damn flip-flop, flirt-or-not attitude. Just to breathe for a second. But he took the step right up to her car, right beside her, so close she couldn't actually open the door.

'So if you're capable of all that bad,' he muttered low in her ear, 'why didn't you have sex with your boyfriend in the back seat of this baby?'

Burning from the inside out, she gave his shoulder a shove—but he didn't move. 'Because it would have been disrespectful,' she answered honestly—and breathlessly.

He spun, leaning back on the door, and getting his face right in hers. 'No more disrespectful than driving round without a licence. How come the cops have never pulled you over?'

She shrugged, battling the urge to lean in the inch that would bring her mouth into contact with his. 'It's a vintage car in mint condition. I think they assume that the dame behind the wheel cares for the car way too much to be doing anything illegal. I always drive carefully.'

'It must be heavy to steer,' he said almost absently, his gaze not releasing hers. 'Who taught you to drive?'

'My grandfather. It was his pride and joy and I respected *him*, so, no, I wasn't going to get spunk stains on the leather.' She'd never have done that to her grandparents. Especially not when her mother had disappointed them with the whole 'baby out of wedlock and left them to hold it' thing.

His smile deepened at her crude reference. 'So why haven't you got the licence?'

'I haven't had the opportunity.'

He looked sceptical. '*How* can you not have had the opportunity?'

'I've been busy,' she fudged. 'Besides, L-plates would ruin the look of the car.'

She'd needed to be able to drive at any time—to get to the urgent pharmacy or wherever when her grandfather's meds ran out. Sure, she could have done it in the last few months, but, yeah, there was that one bit of her that wanted to stick it to the authorities. The institutions that had abandoned her and her family. They'd been left alone to deal with everything. There'd been no support structures. A social-worker visit a long time ago. No follow up. Because by then she was no longer a child— she'd just turned seventeen, her grandmother had just died and left her the sole carer for her grandfather at the beginning of what ended up a long illness. The time she'd needed someone—anyone—to help, there'd been no one.

'You have to get your licence. You can't keep driving without it.'

Who was the Goody Two-Shoes now? Struck her that Gabe had more of a conservative element than anyone had guessed. 'I'm working on it.'

'Getting the celebratory Bolly isn't exactly working on it.' He eyeballed her and looked dead serious. 'Give me the keys.'

She sighed dramatically, covering the hiccup in her heartbeat. 'Who do you think you are?'

Somehow he broadened his position, blocking her from the car door. 'Give me the keys or I'll call the cops and dob you in.'

She gasped at the unmistakable menace in his tone. 'You wouldn't be such a nark.'

'Try me.'

She curled her fingers round the keys so hard they marked her skin.

He just waited, his hand outstretched. 'Give.'

Her nostrils flared as she smacked the keys down hard on his upturned palm.

He straightened and spun, unlocked the car and got into the driver's seat with a wicked grin on his face as he unwound the window to talk to her. 'I've always wanted to drive one of these. Can I drive home?'

She glared at him looking so at home in her 1954 Mark 1 Zephyr with its powder-blue base and gleaming chrome. No way was he driving her baby. 'What about your own car?' It was one of those sporty convertible things that cost an absolute fortune. Parked only a few spots away from hers, it was too flash for daylight.

He reached into his pocket and threw his keys at her. 'You drive it.'

She was so shocked she failed to catch them. 'No way.' She picked the keys from the ground, balled her fists and stuck them on her hips.

'Why not?' He laughed, annoyingly. And, yes, reheating those parts that always leapt to life in his presence. The melt was almost impossible to prevent now.

'Because it's worth eighty times what mine is,' she fumed, trying to stay mad with him, trying not to like him all the more for teasing her so hard. 'I drive that and you're not insured. I can't afford any bill to fix a dent in your baby.'

He leaned back in the seat, a smug expression all over. 'Goody Two-Shoes.'

'Fine, so what if I am?'

'You *stay* that way.' His eyes flashed as he got out of the car and handed her keys back to her. 'You know, you really should get your licence,' he said condescendingly. 'You're not covered by insurance without it. One day you'll get caught and then you'll get done. You don't want a conviction to ruin your chances of getting an entry visa into the US or wherever it is you want to go travelling to, do you?'

She frowned, not pleased by that idea. 'Could that happen?'

He shrugged. 'Dunno. Maybe.' He held the door for her, way too close again as she took up position in the driver's seat. 'Guess you'd better drive carefully...' He trailed off and then dipped down to murmur slyly, 'Unless you want me to drive you?'

Oh, now there was no holding back on the flirt of it. Not when he couldn't help himself either. She turned her head and peered up at him, fluttering her lashes. 'Gabe, you know I want you to drive,' she cooed. 'Just not my car.'

He chuckled as he shut the door, then reached through the window to gently brush her jaw with his knuckles. 'Keep working on the sass, I'm sure one day you'll graduate to fully frisky vixen.'

She glared at him and started the engine. 'Better stand back, the steering on this beast can be tricky sometimes, wouldn't want to run over your toes.'

He followed her home, making her so hot and bothered she missed a couple of gear changes. A glance in her rear-view mirror showed the flash of his smile in the car too close behind hers. She turned into her place, got out to drag open the heavy old garage door, then parked her car inside.

He'd parked on the street, so she left the garage door

open for him. He walked in and shut it with annoying ease. Then he walked to where she was trying to straighten the blue tarpaulin that barely covered the towers of cardboard boxes she'd stacked along the back wall.

'You have so much stuff,' he commented as she turned towards him.

'Yeah, but at least it's all sorted now.' She glanced back at the boxes with displeasure. 'I'm not sure what to do with it.'

'You don't want to keep it?'

'Not all of it. But if I let it go, then it's gone for good.' All the memories, the stories, their lives. She'd been through every inch and not found the answers she wanted. 'Same with the furniture.' She sighed and walked to the small door that led out to the garden. 'I got rid of a few things, but you've seen the rest all jammed in up there.' And she couldn't bring herself to get rid of it.

'There's no one else who might want some of it?' he asked as he followed her.

'No. My mother was an only child. So was I.' No aunts and uncles, no cousins. She was the only one left in her little family.

'What about your father?'

Roxie hardened her heart enough to be able to answer lightly. 'I don't know anything about him.'

'Not even his name?' he joked.

But she couldn't do more than answer baldly then. 'No.'

'Oh.' He cleared his throat and looked anywhere but at her. 'Sorry.'

'It's okay.' Now she felt sorry for making him feel awkward. She shouldn't have said anything but she felt as if she had to explain more now—to ease over the moment. 'There aren't any records. No clues in any of those boxes. Naturally no bureaucratic department is able to help either.' She forced a smile. They never seemed to be able to help her.

He met her eyes and half smiled back. 'So this was your mum's house?'

'No, she lived in the UK. I was raised by my grand-parents. This is their house.'

'And they left it to you?'

She nodded.

'When?'

Oh, man, hadn't they covered enough already? He didn't know it but he was dragging the conversation to even boggier ground. But she maintained her smile and quickly recited the facts. 'My grandmother died when I was sixteen. My grandfather died just over a year ago.'

'I'm sorry.' He turned slightly away and looked at the beautiful house, which was good because holding her smile was causing mouth ache. 'Where's your mum now?'

Roxie closed her eyes for a split second. 'She died when I was eight.'

'Man,' he muttered softly. 'That's rough.'

Roxie shrugged and downplayed it. 'She lived over-seas. I grew up with my grandparents so I didn't know her that well. I've lived here all my life.'

Long ago she had mourned for what could have been, as a kid she'd been filled with the idealistic hope that her mother would one day return to her and would answer all her deep-held questions. But that hadn't happened and any chance of getting those answers had been bur-ied with the last of her family. She'd spent the year sort-ing through papers, sorting through those feelings. Now she'd put them all into boxes and sealed them away.

She glanced at him and saw the one thing she'd never seen from anyone else. The one thing she *didn't* want to see from him.

'I don't need sympathy, Gabe,' she said, annoyed by it. 'A year or so ago, it would have been nice.' And she couldn't help throwing him the challenge that one last time. 'What I need now is some fun and adventure. It's been a long time coming.' There was no soft coo, or coy look this time, she spoke with hard, raw honesty.

'I don't think diving off the deep end is the way to go,' he answered with clipped finality.

Roxie couldn't believe it—so the flirt of mere minutes ago had just been that? He was still denying this? So much for him being the ultimate slayer. He'd come over all old-school gallant because of that one stupid word—virgin. She had no idea how he'd got that playboy reputation; it truly was misplaced. And she was mortified because she'd thrown herself so hard at him.

'You don't think I can handle it? I've handled more than you can ever imagine.' But she sure as hell wasn't going to give him the fine details of her sob story to gain points like some try-hard on a reality TV talent show. She was mad with herself for saying the bit she had already. Sympathy *really* wasn't what she wanted.

He looked at her too intently for another too long moment, his stance rigid. 'I'll see you at the game tomorrow.' His parting words came over his shoulder as he strode away. 'Dance hard.'

CHAPTER FIVE

ROXIE pulled on her costume, engulfed by embarrassment. Gabe was avoiding her. She'd seen him duck his head back from the window when she'd been out in the garden this morning and he'd immediately zipped the other way when he'd seen her down the corridor at the stadium as she'd arrived half an hour before. So, yeah, she'd made a huge mistake. He wasn't interested at all—had merely been flirting for amusement. And now he knew some of her history he was probably afraid she was all fragile and about to go crazy like his ex.

'Almost ready?' Chelsea asked with a bouncy flick of her hair.

Roxie nodded and bent to smooth her outfit so she could hide her face. Yep, she should have paid closer attention to Chelsea's warning. If it weren't for the fact that she didn't have her funds together yet, she'd be on the next plane.

And now there was this. Her first night dancing as a Silver Blade. She stared at her reflection, trying to tell herself that if she didn't recognise herself, no one else would, and therefore it wouldn't matter if she made a total dork of herself on the pitch. Only she was terrified—all her confidence and self-belief sucked away. *What* did she think she *was* doing? She was going to

make a total fool of herself. She didn't have the experience or the training for this. And as she frowned at the
mirror she realised she couldn't remember the start of
their first routine. She'd gone totally blank. She tried
to breathe but she needed fresh air—not the clouds of
hairspray in the Blades' change room. The fumes were
stinging her eyes.

Gabe was almost ready for the game. He'd strapped a
couple of players' knees for extra support, had his kit
ready for sideline duty. But his head was somewhere
else altogether—repeatedly banging on the brick wall
of desire. He was out of his mind for that provocative,
beautiful woman so out of bounds. He went for a walk,
determined to claw back the necessary focus. Striding
along the corridor, he almost missed the shadow lurking
at the back of a remote stairwell. He did a double take,
but his body recognised her immediately. 'Roxie? What
are you doing here?'

'Nothing. Having a moment. Go away.' The last of
her breathless comments rose. Kind of like a question
but more like hysteria.

'No.' He moved closer, answering her firmly. 'You're
upset. What's wrong?' Adrenalin surged, his muscles
flooded with aggression-filled strength. 'Has one of the
players done something?'

'What? No!'

He believed her, but he also heard the raw emotion
cracking her voice. He'd seen plenty of fear in his job
and he saw it in her now. The way she was clutching her
hands together, as if she was trying to stop herself flee-
ing. Beneath the silver glitter her eyes were wide with
terror.

Concern gripped him. 'Please tell me what's wrong.'

He couldn't breathe, holding himself back from drawing her hard against him so he could keep her safe from whatever, wherever, the danger was.

'I'm fine. Really. Just having a breather. Lots of perfume in that room, you know?'

She was babbling. Why was she babbling?

'I wanted a walk. You know. Clear the head.' She looked at him with eyes so huge they were manic. 'I'm nervous.'

Finally he could release the screaming tension in his lungs. He was so relieved, but he knew better than to laugh at her. 'You're a great dancer. You'll be fine.'

She shook her head violently, her hair streaming out like a gold and bronze waterfall. 'I've never done it before.'

He groaned. 'Roxie, now is not the time to talk—'

'No.' She actually managed a laugh. 'Not that. I've never danced in front of an audience.'

'What?' She had to be kidding. Never danced before an audience?

She was still talking—faster and faster. 'The stadium is full. And there's the broadcast—all those viewers at home. I've not been to a dance class in *years*. I did ballet as a girl but when Grandma had the stroke, I gave up classes. I'm self-taught from dance vids and music clips. I'm not good enough to be alongside those professionally trained girls with all their experience. Who am I kidding? I can't do it.'

'Yes, you can.' Gabe's head was spinning with all that info, with a ton more questions.

But she just shook her head wildly, her body trembling, on the edge of making a run for it.

'Just imagine you're in the garden and there's no one there.' He stepped closer and kept his voice calm. 'You dance incredibly in the garden.' He'd watched her so often, he knew how damn well she moved. A million times better than any of those other girls—she totally had edge.

She looked even more panicked. 'I can't do it.'

Fear was irrational. And it was obvious his rational attempt to reassure wasn't going to work. But he wasn't about to tranquillise her, which left only one course of action—distraction.

And this was purely to offer comfort, right? There was comfort in a cuddle. That was all it would be. He could manage that and only that. For sure. Because there was no way he couldn't touch her now. He didn't have the strength not to. Didn't have the desire not to. All that mattered was making her feel that little bit better.

Roxie was almost in tears. Trying so hard to blink them back because she was going to ruin her make-up if they spilt over. And she hadn't cried in months—she couldn't cry over something as silly as this. She held her hands together, pressing them tight just below her ribs. Wanting to stop shaking, unable to control her agitated movements. The more she tried to calm down, the more upset she got. And having him here wasn't helping. She'd been getting a grip 'til now. Now she was all over the place. She wanted him to clear off. Only now he'd moved right in front of her.

'Roxie.' He gripped her shoulders hard.

Startled, she lifted her head to look into his face.

'Roxie,' he said again, the tone of his voice totally changing.

Her whole system froze for a moment and then slowly focused on him. But he didn't say anything more, just the smallest of smiles appeared on his face. Fascinated, she watched, because that smile wasn't one she'd seen from him before—that smile was full of naughtiness, full of promise. His eyes reflected it, darkening with only a slim gleam shining from the very centre. She held her breath as his expression deepened wickedly. It looked as if the rake in him had been released.

One hand released her shoulder, moving close to cup her jaw, his broad palm pressed almost the length of her throat. He held her firmly. Her breathing slowed as she watched him move so slowly nearer. His touch seemed to drug her, replacing the anxiety twitching through her veins with a sluggish warmth instead. She couldn't move—not to encourage, or to run away. She could only wait. And want.

His thumb moved, stroking, the pressure of his fingers increasing on the vulnerable pulse point in her neck. She felt the release of his breath over her face. Her eyelids fluttered, blocking the visual overload from him being so close, so her body could focus on the touch, the scent.

His kiss was soft and not anywhere near enough to her lips. She felt the pull deep within—the ember that had been smouldering for so long was blown into a flame with just those too few touches.

'You're going to be amazing,' he whispered, almost crooning, as his lips touched her skin. 'Just amazing.' He kissed along her jaw. 'You are amazing.'

Heat flooded her system, galvanising her again—only this time the energy pulsing through her was born not of fear, but of desire. She wanted closer, wanted to cling. The one thing she'd wanted for days was now in front of her. Teasing, tormenting, captivating—just out of reach.

'Go out and have fun,' he said.

She didn't care about the damn dancing any more. The fun was right here.

'Kiss me,' she said softly.

He did, but not where she wanted. Another series of kisses down her throat. He brushed the swathe of hair from her neck, clearing the path for his lips with skilful strokes of his fingertips.

She leaned closer, felt one hand at her back as he adjusted to take her weight, crushing her to his length. She threw her head back, abandoned, as he pressed ever more passionate kisses across her skin. His teeth nipped, his tongue flickered to soothe the tiny scratches, his hands held. She discovered just how much she loved to be held by him. How much she'd wanted it. She yielded to him completely.

'Roxie,' his tone warned, his voice rasping.

Her body burned for more. 'Kiss me properly.' She wanted his mouth on hers. She wanted to be absorbed entirely in his embrace.

She could feel the acceleration in his breathing as his abdomen was sealed to hers, could feel the hunger rising as his kisses swooped lower, across her chest, down to the curve of her amplified breasts. He licked down the deep vee of her Lycra top. She felt the hardening in his body as hers softened—his bulging erection insistent against her belly.

'Gabe,' she begged.

He dragged his mouth from her skin. 'I'll kiss you properly after the show.' A hot, rough mutter.

Her heart banged. 'No.' She rolled her hips against his, teasing the only way she could. 'Now.'

Both his hands gripped her butt, holding her still— flush against his strained jeans. 'After.'

'No,' she sighed, rubbing against him. The tiniest of

movements that his grip allowed, but enough to send her to the brink of ecstasy. 'Please.'

'You're going to be late,' he groaned, his mouth dropping to her collarbone again, his pelvis rocking powerfully against hers. 'You can't be late.'

'Don't stop.' She didn't care how desperate she sounded.

He moved against her once more, his kisses frantic on her skin, his groan harsh in her ears. Her nipples screamed for his mouth to cover them, the hunger in her womb was all heat. Oh, she wanted him, wanted, wanted, wanted.

'Please kiss me,' she begged. 'Please.'

But then, with a set jaw he stepped back. '*After* the show.'

Panting, she couldn't believe it. She shook her head, but was too breathless to plead more. He took her upper arm in a firm grip and walked, swiftly guiding her back down the corridor towards the changing room. He pushed the door open but kept walking—leaving her.

'There you are!' Chelsea called from inside. 'I was wondering.'

Roxie had no choice but to go in. So warm, so excited, so amazed. Slowly her smile spread. He'd changed his mind. He was hers. No way could he deny them now. She'd felt the way he shook for her, how hard, how strong his hunger was.

'Ready?' Chelsea asked. 'You look great.'

A quick glance in the mirror showed sparkling eyes, her cheeks glowing. Blood racing. Every cell singing in excitement. And her make-up still perfect.

'I am *so* ready.' She beamed. She couldn't wait for it to be over.

In the distance, the music thumped, amping the crowd

higher. She heard the calls, the whistles. She laughed aloud as they ran through the tunnel and out onto the pitch. The noise burst into her. It was crazy, it was fun and it was only the beginning. She moved fast, her body fluid, free, totally relaxed, zinging on the anticipation. She'd never loved dancing so much. Never felt so aware of her body.

She wasn't aware of anyone watching her, the crowd a distant blur, and inside her mind she saw only him, his breathlessness, his dark eyes gleaming beneath half-closed lashes. She danced thinking of nothing and no one but him, of his expression as he'd moved closer, of the way he'd seemed to savour every touch of her skin. Being that desired was incredibly intoxicating. And the heady pleasure released her from any anxiety, any self-consciousness. She danced only for him and for herself.

During the game she knelt on the sideline with the other dancers. For this part they held pompoms, which they were to shake and shimmy at high points in the game—i.e. when the boys scored. Which they frequently did. She was loving it now—looking forward to dancing more at half-time. All nerves eviscerated.

She knew exactly where Gabe was—impossible to miss him with his neon green vest over his jeans and DOCTOR printed in large lettering across the back. Far sexier than the numbers on the rugby pitch. He ran on a couple of times to deal with blood injuries. She saw him moving to ice a couple of boys' knees and ankles when fresh players were subbed on in the second half. She was so aware of him, felt such a connection, it was a wonder the world couldn't see the string attached from her eyes to him.

After the game—which naturally the Knights won—she wriggled out of her costume and into her new dress.

The kind of thing she'd never have worn when her grand-father was around to see it. Not that it was low cut, but it clung in all the right places—to the curves that she'd let go back to almost normal in just a booster bra rather than all-out padded. False advertising wasn't necessary for Gabe, he already knew what was on offer and, to her great pleasure, he still wanted. There was an after-match function within the stadium and then most of the players and dancers went to a particular club in town. Her first time to attend. But she'd happily skip it. She couldn't wait to be alone with Gabe—to finally get the kiss she'd been waiting for for ever. And then everything else.

She walked into the crowded room with a couple of the other dancers, her smile impossible to contain. She searched, her eyes flickering from one tall man to the next. Her heart beat louder, drowning the noise of talk and laughter and clinking glasses. Icy awareness slith-ered down her spine. She was certain before she'd even finished her sweep of the room.

Gabe had gone.

CHAPTER SIX

ROXIE ran up the stairs to her tiny bedsit above the garage, too defiant to bother about being quiet. There was no light on in the house so maybe he was still out. Maybe she'd missed him somehow and he was still at the bar waiting for her.

But she knew he wasn't. She'd stayed for the drinks, gone on to the club and danced her heart out in the crowd, pretending she didn't care that the coward had chickened out of following through with her. He was still treating her like someone not old enough or cool enough or sophisticated enough to be with him.

So now, nearly two in the morning, she unwound the wire cage on the P-for-performance bottle of Bolly. Stood in her open doorway and fired the cork towards his house. Then was crass enough to drink straight from the bottle.

It tasted good.

She was hot and thirsty, both angered and excited, sleep was utterly impossible. So standing on the landing out in the warm night air, swigging from a bottle that was emptying surprisingly quickly, seemed like a damn fine idea. She glared over at his house, mentally rehearsing what she was going to say to him as soon as she saw him again. With every sip she grew more riled, more defiant, more confident.

Damn the man.

She had a key to his house. After all, it was *her* house. And he was so going to get a piece of her mind. He owed her. Why shouldn't she go in now and let him know all about it?

She ditched the drained bottle and grabbed her keys, kicking off her shoes before skipping down the stairs and along the path that led to his back door. She unlocked it and stepped inside. Realised then that she didn't know which room he'd taken. No matter, the house was hardly huge.

She walked into the master bedroom downstairs. The one with the en suite where he'd washed out her eyes. Nothing.

Which left only the bedroom upstairs on the mezzanine floor—her old room. The door was ajar; she nudged it open. He hadn't drawn the curtains and living in the central city meant there was a lot of light pollution, so she could see quite well—especially with the full moonlight streaming in as well.

She stared at the bed. The bastard was sound asleep. How the hell could he be sound asleep when she was being eaten alive by fantasies of everything she wanted to do to him—and for him to do to her?

Without thinking she walked closer, because it was a hot night and he was sleeping with just a sheet covering him. No pjs or tee shirt or vest or anything. Just a sheet that was currently resting low round his hips. She drank in the sight of his bare chest, breathed deep as she scoped his ripped abs.

He stirred and opened his eyes. Took a glimpse of her

and groaned, closing his eyes tight. 'F...in' dreamin'...
Rox...'

Enthralled, she watched as he groaned her name
again, watched his hand slide below that sheet to where
it was seriously rucked up. He sighed then, frustration
seeking satisfaction.

O-o-okay-yay-yay-yay.

She smiled broadly, thrilled to know she wasn't alone
in dealing with explicit dreams. She reached forward and
trailed a finger down his sternum towards his belly button. 'I'm right here.'

'What the...!' He sat bolt upright, his hand slamming
on top of hers, squashing it against his chest so she could
feel his heart thumping right through her fingers.

'Roxie?' His eyes horrified wide. 'What the hell are
you doing here?'

She tried to tug her hand free but he didn't let it go.
He glared, his chest rising and falling as if he'd been
sprinting.

She glared back. 'You ran out on me.'

'Roxie...' He flung her hand from him. 'You can't
just break into someone's house.'

'For the record, this is *my* house. But don't panic,' she
drawled sarcastically. 'I'm not here to attack you or move
in on you. I just want to give you a piece of my mind.'

He puffed out a big breath. 'It couldn't wait 'til morning?'

'No, because you acted like a jerk.'

'No, I didn't,' he snapped back. 'I was very nice and
helped calm your nerves.'

'Oh, like they taught you that in med school? Don't
try to act like it wasn't something *you* instigated. And
don't try to pretend it wasn't something you've wanted

for days. And don't you dare try to pretend nothing more personal isn't going to happen.'

He shifted. The sheet slipped. He hastily pulled it back.

Yeah, his 'personal' reaction was only getting bigger. And she was beyond sure of him now. Anticipation licked her nerves and made her laugh. 'Did you know there's over two hundred and fifty million bubbles in a bottle of champagne? Which means there are about a hundred and twenty-five million bubbles zinging through my veins now.'

Gabe leaned back and rested his head back on the headboard, his pulse still settling from the shock of waking to find her in his room. But this reality was no nightmare, just pure fantasy—a too-pretty girl laughing at him, daring him, tempting him. 'Someone bothered to count?' he drawled, trying to feign some cool—some control.

'Apparently so.'

'You've had your bottle, then?'

'All by myself.' She sniffed. 'You should have had some with me.'

He shook his head slowly, ruefully smiling. He'd lick the last drops from her lips given half the chance. But the trouble was he *liked* her. And that was where the complications arose. He sensed hurt beneath her determinedly sunny exterior, was certain she was denying loneliness and who knew what other needs. But he couldn't ever be the guy to give security. His lifestyle would never accommodate a serious relationship and he didn't want emotional hassle. It had taken him too long to feel his own freedom. And he couldn't trust that she wouldn't think she wanted more if they became fully intimate.

'No matter.' She sashayed closer. 'You promised me something.'

Oh, the temptation was extreme now. 'I didn't promise,' he muttered weakly.

'After the show.' She ignored his denial. 'I danced how you said to. Did you see?'

His gaze dropped to the sheet as he tried so hard to expunge the image that had sprung to mind. 'Yes.'

'Did you like it?' Her voice went husky.

He swallowed. This was torture. Utter torture.

'You're afraid to answer that?'

'Yes,' he admitted.

'Why?'

'I don't want to hurt you.'

'You won't. So long as I'm warmed up—and I do believe I am.' She chuckled. 'It shouldn't hurt that much at all, should it? I always figured the pain thing was a way of trying to put a girl off. Trying to keep us "good",' She gurgled with laughter.

'Roxie.' He felt strangled as heat consumed him. 'I didn't mean physically.'

'Oh.' She bit her lip but the giggle continued anyway.

'I'm serious.' He sat upright, angry and frustrated and so, *so* painfully hard. 'Can you really do a one-night stand, Roxie? Can you really stay emotionally disconnected? First lovers usually go hand in hand with first *love*—involving more emotions than you intend simply because you don't have the experience to control them. I don't want emotional entanglement. I don't want commitment. If we did this it would matter more to you than it would to me.'

'No, it wouldn't,' she denied it. 'All that matters to me is having it good and I know it'll be that way with you.'

He screwed his eyes shut tight, because he knew it

would be so much *more* than good. 'You're a virgin. A *drunk* virgin,' he reminded himself. 'What am I thinking trying to have this conversation now? Get the hell out of here.'

'I'm not drunk,' she asserted bluntly. 'I want you. And I don't want anything more than tonight.'

His eyes shot open and he took a deep, pained gulp for sanity.

'Isn't it every man's fantasy to initiate a woman in the art of sensual pleasure?' She sighed with the most witchery smile he'd ever seen. 'Why not show me how good it can be?'

He'd been hard for her since the moment he'd found her red-eyed scrubbing the shower—long before she'd told him her secret. But her devastating frankness—that mix of innocence and carnal desire—made him want her all the more. Hell, yes, he wanted to show her how good it could be. But he couldn't. He just couldn't.

Wild with both her and himself, he threw off the sheet and swung out of bed.

Open-mouthed, Roxie gazed as he stood up. He was hotter than she'd imagined. His abs rippled beneath golden skin and a smattering of dark hair that arrowed down to emphasise the huge hard-on he was packing. He advanced towards her with aggression inked all over him. Some of her bubbles popped. 'What are you doing?'

'Frogmarching you home. Leaving you there. Alone.'

But his body gave him away. And they both knew it. She shook her head. 'I never should have told you.'

'No, I'm glad you told me. I can stop us both making a big mistake.'

Emboldened by that skyscraper of an erection, she walked up to him. 'How can it be a mistake, Gabe? When we both want it? I'm not a complete novice. I know how to stroke this.'

This time she went straight for the kill—couldn't resist the chance to hold. She cupped his balls, let her fingers feather up his shaft, let her thumb rub over the broad tip. Oh, she felt dizzy now.

His hand tangled in her hair, fingers twisting in the strands and then tugging to pull her head back. Mouth open, breathing hard, she gazed up at him through half-closed lids. Unashamedly his to manipulate however he wanted.

She heard him swear, the words so violently uttered she felt the wind gust over her face. Then he crushed her mouth beneath his.

Finally.

She'd been dreaming of this for days. And for once reality was better than dreams. No soft caress, it was all erotic, all consuming and carnal. She shook with the violence of need that erupted within her, with the violence of his kiss. She pushed through the initial shock of passion to move closer, deeper into him. Not wanting him to think she couldn't handle all he could give. Because she knew she could, now she wanted it all— with a fury that might have frightened her had she been one hundred per cent herself. But the last hint of caution had been drowned—bubbles flowed through her veins, effervescent, exhilarating, exquisite. And not the champagne; not the alcohol. Pure joy at being this close to someone. This one person, whose simple presence could set off an uncontrollable, instinctive reaction within her. And now he was where she'd wanted him most—pouring his fiery energy and focus on her. Desperately she strained, her tongue lashing with his, shivering in his embrace yet wanting closer. She curled one leg around his, bringing her pelvis into direct contact with his. But it wasn't enough. It still wasn't enough.

Gabe's hands clenched hard on her body when he felt her leg slide around his, when he felt her core. Even through her knickers he felt the dampness. The evidence of how ready for him she was.

He nearly lost his mind. And it really didn't help that she was lapping up the kiss that he knew was too rough. He forced himself to ease off, to be a little more gentle. At the very least he could do that for her.

But she mewled, her chin lifting, her lips catching his again—her tongue assaulting his mouth, her hands taking him in a too tight clutch. She was as rough as he.

'Gabe.' It was a demand for everything.

Frustration made him shake, until he grabbed her butt in his hands and lifted her, carrying her to his bed. He lay her back on it, lay on her. Taking pleasure in the groaning sigh she gave as he let her take the bulk of his weight. He rose a little on his elbows so his pelvis ground harder into hers.

Her pupils dilated. He saw the blood beating its rosy path to her cheeks, her lips. There was no denying she wanted it—*him*. She arched, her hips thrusting. Inexperienced she might be, but she had all the right instincts.

Gabe bent his head and kissed her, letting them both drown in the powerful pleasure of it again. His head spinning at how good it felt to be with her like this. But the alarm in the back of his brain was ringing louder and louder and louder. If he did this now, he wouldn't be able to live with himself. She'd been drinking and he hadn't. But he couldn't not touch her. He ached to satisfy her. Ached to satisfy himself. Only the former was allowed.

Even then he enforced limited options on himself. He wasn't going to take advantage of her condition. She wasn't sure of all she was offering. Her defences were totally down—thanks to some expensive champagne. It was not okay to take her at her word.

But the way she moved was just killing him. The way she kissed. Passionate and hungry. She rubbed against him, hitching her dress so they could lie skin to skin.

He buried his face in her neck, all his weight pinning her now, his cock straining to push through the thin barriers between them. He could feel her tiny movements, the friction an intense, intolerable tease.

How was he supposed to resist her sighs and pleas and writhing body? How was he supposed to deny her the pleasure she sought?

He shifted, forcing himself away, keeping her in place with a heavy thigh rather than his whole body. He kissed her and swept his hand up under her skirt, finding those lace-edged knickers so quickly, sliding beneath them with even greater ease. He moaned into her mouth as he felt the hot wetness. Then he focused. Stroked. The lightest brush with the tip of his finger against the small nub that would send her into orbit if he did it right.

Seemed he did it right because her moan then, was the pure sound of sensual pleasure. He felt the throb as blood pulsed, swelling her sex, feminine moisture slicking her more—preparing her for his invasion. He ached to plunge his fingers deep, his shaft, his whole damn self. So desperately he wanted to bury deep inside her and ride hard and furious to an orgasm he knew would be out of this world. Because *she* was out of this world, the most beautiful, passionate woman.

His frustrated passion found release in her mouth. He rammed his tongue deep and rhythmic. Barely a kiss, more a brutal display of unbridled desire. But she took it, her neck arching, her whole body arching, making herself more accessible, more vulnerable to him. Even more impossible to resist. But he did—refusing to possess her sex, just touching her sweet spot so, so lightly. He pulled back the urgency of the kiss too—worked hard to play more, to tease her more. As she arched higher still her hands raked his back. He almost burst out of his skin, had never felt lust as painful as this. His heart hammered, his skin coated with sweat even though he was barely moving. Holding back required the most extreme effort of his life.

He felt her scream as those exquisite sensations shuddered through her, but he wouldn't release her from his kiss, nor from the soft strokes of his finger back and forth and round and round. Not entering her, just rubbing, rubbing, rubbing, teasing that pulsing nub mercilessly. She shook, her body taut and then trembling as the orgasm tumbled her into those moments of mindlessness. He persevered, relentless in his need to wring it all from her, to exhaust her. Her fingernails scratched hard. He pressed her deeper into the bed. His mouth pleasuring hers until she went completely lax.

Only then did he ease back, pulling her to her side to cradle her from behind, trying to regulate his breathing and the unbearable agony inside.

'Oh, Gabe,' she breathed. A sound filled with satisfaction.

'Shh.' He stroked her hair, pulled her dress back down over her thighs and waited for sleep to claim her.

Mercifully it wasn't long before it did. And then she was a warm soft bundle in his bed. And he couldn't move. His swollen cock was so sensitive even the brush of the cotton sheet above him hurt it. He gritted his teeth, willing it to subside. But lay awake for hours tormenting himself with visions of what he could have done, once would have done without a second thought.

Having a conscience really sucked.

CHAPTER SEVEN

WHEN Roxie woke she was alone. She blinked at the familiar walls. She was in her room—she'd woken up every morning here for almost her entire life.

Only now she remembered. Now it was all different.

She lifted the sheet, saw she still wore her dress, her underwear. She dropped the sheet and slumped back down on the pillow. Gabe wasn't there, of course. And she remembered it all. The ferocious kisses, the feel of his weight, the way he'd touched her until she'd come.

But that had been all.

But, damn it, it wasn't going to be all any more. Now she knew he dreamed of her just as she did him. So there was to be no more pretending otherwise. She wriggled out of her dress, knickers and bra. She refused to leave his bed until he'd come as hard as she had. It was only fair, after all. So she lay back and waited. Trying not to lose her nerve.

Fortunately, she didn't have to wait long. He appeared in the doorway in dark jeans and nothing else. She figured he'd taken a shower given his hair was damp, his jaw clean-shaven. But he still managed to exude edginess—the grump was back.

'Have you got a headache?' he asked roughly.

'No,' she answered sweetly, stifling the butterflies in her stomach. 'I wasn't drunk, Gabe.'

He cleared his throat and looked to the left of her. 'Are you hungry?'

'Yes,' she said with determined sass, totally not meaning what he'd meant.

He shot a heated glare at her.

She smiled wider, because she wanted to get to him, she wanted to push him over his damn boundaries. 'I remember everything.'

He looked so uncomfortable then that Roxie's anger began to bite. If he dared apologise she was going to have to hurt him.

'You were tipsy,' he said firmly. 'I'm sorry. I shouldn't have…' His voice trailed off.

Her turn to send a glare—an unforgiving look from top to—*oh*.

Yeah, that was when she noticed that he was hard. That the bulge in the front of his jeans was nowhere near normal size. That his lickable nipples were taut. That despite the heat of the morning, there were goosebumps peppering his skin.

Her flash of anger fled and amusement—*elation*—emboldened her. She sat up, clutching the sheet to her chest for a last second as she got out of the bed. Once standing, she let the sheet fall.

'Gabe,' she murmured. As she walked towards him she ran her hands down her sides and let her hips sway. Her whole body was ready to sway with his.

He stared, his mouth open, frozen to the spot.

That reaction was all she needed to lose every last inhibition. 'You really don't need to feel bad about doing something that I'd already done to myself.'

His eyes widened, darkened, heated. His mouth shut

then opened again before shutting a final time. Clearly rendered speechless. Dull colour washed over his cheekbones. It was the first time Roxie had seen a man blush.

She got within touch distance and let her amusement warm her whisper. 'I've been thinking about you a lot.'

'What were you doing when you were thinking about me?' he answered, completely hoarse.

She ran her tongue along her lips and smiled.

Almost helplessly, he lifted his hands, held them just in front of her. 'What did you imagine these were doing when you were thinking of me?'

She took them in her own and guided them towards her body. Placed one on her breast. His fingers automatically moved to cup her flesh, to graze over her tight nipple. His other hand she placed palm down on her belly and covered it with her own. Slowly she pushed their fingers down and down.

'What did you dream I would do?' he whispered.

'Everything,' she murmured, shifting so her feet were slightly further apart. 'I imagined everything.'

'Hell, Roxie,' he muttered. 'How am I supposed to resist you?'

She smiled. 'You're not.'

'Every time I close my eyes, you're here,' he confessed. His fingers teased—her nipple, her sex.

Her eyes were half closed now as she shivered. 'Does the reality live up to the dream?'

'I'll make it,' he promised. 'I'll do that for you.'

'You did last night,' she said. 'But I'm taking it all today, Gabe.'

She threaded her fingers through his hair and held him still as she reached up and kissed him.

In a second he claimed dominance, crushing her mouth beneath his. Instantly as carnal and passionate and furious as last night. His tongue impolite, demanding, his hands hauling her closer, the denim rough on her naked skin.

'Are you sure you can handle this,' he demanded, breathing heavily.

She leaned closer, resting her weight on him. 'I want more.'

She wasn't afraid of the strength rippling through him. The way he'd shown her that passion unleashed last night. She liked it. Her mouth felt huge from the pressure of the kiss just now. All she wanted was another one.

'More,' she muttered again, reaching onto tiptoe to press her lips to his again. More, more, more.

Sunlight streamed through the windows. There was no need for the duvet. He threw back the coverings leaving only the sheet-clad mattress and pillows beneath them. She reached round his waist from behind and unfastened his jeans. She pushed them—and the boxers beneath—down. Her hand cupping him for only a second before he spun to face her, to seize her wrists.

She liked seeing him naked in broad daylight. Able to watch the movement of strong muscles beneath golden skin. To feel the focus in his now pure-black eyes. To taste the sparkle as sweat slicked his skin. And she was so hot.

He tumbled her to the bed—thankfully, because her legs had lost all boldness now. He kissed her mouth, her face, her neck, then back to her mouth again as if he couldn't bear to leave it for long. His hands swept down her body, stroking every over-sensitive spot with teasing touches—alternately light and firm. She couldn't bear to wait much longer. So wanting—so wanton—and ready.

But he peeled away from her. She gasped, panicking. 'Don't leave me now. Don't you dare stop.'

'I'm not strong enough to stop,' he muttered, his gaze fiercely scraping down her naked body. 'Not again.'

The passionate look in his eyes sent tremors along her nerves. 'Gabe.'

He swiftly reached under the bed, struggled to rip the plastic wrap sealing the box of condoms. She sat up and watched as he rolled it down his erection. He glanced up and caught her. She smiled. He smiled back.

Yeah, happiness surged as she realised he'd laid down his weapons. He couldn't deny it any more and she no longer had to fight him for it.

He pinned her to the bed with his weight. 'There's no going back now.'

'Good.' She wasn't afraid.

He kissed her, his knees pushing her legs further apart as he settled over her. Excited, she wriggled closer. She could feel him, heavy, thick, just out of reach. Her heart thudded and she clasped his shoulders, pressing kisses on his jaw. He put his other hand between them, his fingers seeking her first, teasing in circles, while he kissed a burning trail from one breast to the other, until she was breathing hard and wet and rocking to an ever-increasing rhythm, urgently needing that satisfaction.

'I don't want to come without you,' she panted, desperate for him to take her.

He grazed the soft swell of her breast with his teeth. 'You can come again with me.'

She arched, rigid, on the brink of release. 'No, I want all of you now,' she begged.

'Don't limit yourself,' he muttered. 'Indulge.'

It was too late to deny it anyway. Ecstasy slammed into her. She shuddered, lost in the intensity of the tumbling sensations. Her fingers curled into his broad shoulders as she convulsed, desperate still to draw him closer.

As her screams ebbed he encouraged, his voice thick with satisfaction, his words hot and thrilling. 'Now you're going to come again.'

Panting, she shook her head, certain it was impossible.

'Yes,' he muttered. 'Think yes.'

He shifted, so he was no longer touching her intimately, lifting his hands to toy with her nipples instead, pressing kisses to the vulnerable pulse points on her neck. Keeping her in the moan zone but carefully not touching where she was too sensitive. Not yet. And slowly that hazy giddiness receded as she became aware of need knifing through her—even more urgent than before.

'Yes,' she repeated his mutter. Anticipation, energy flooded back—nothing but erotic hunger in her body. She rocked her hips up to his, seeking his touch there again. Now.

Wickedly he smiled. 'Oh, yes.' He kissed her, his mouth and tongue staking the claim the rest of him was about to.

His hand moved between them again. She felt him gently rubbing, only this time it wasn't his fingers, but the head of his erection sliding back and forth at the entrance of her slick folds, spreading her damp signs of delight, almost, almost becoming part of her. She sucked in air but it did nothing to cool her. She rocked harder, trying to force him to hurry, but he just chuckled. She ran her hand down his back, clutched his butt, urging him closer, while her other hand pushed into his hair, pulling him back for another of those possessive, passionate kisses. She moaned, so excited by his teasing strokes, so on the edge of her next orgasm.

His hands framed her face and he captured her gaze

with a searching one of his own as he slowly, smoothly claimed her.

She closed her eyes at the intensity of it. Tremors racking her body, her mouth opening in an involuntary, silent sigh.

His movement ceased completely.

'Gabe?' She looked at him, startled by the expression of pain on his face.

'It's not right that something that feels so good for me should be hurting you,' he whispered gruffly.

'It's not hurting,' she breathed. 'Honest it's not. It feels…' She paused to consider whether saying 'overwhelming' would be wise or not. But as she deliberated he tensed, and suddenly all thought fled. 'Do that again,' she demanded.

'Do what?' He looked agonised.

'Move like that again.'

He tensed, pressing that touch closer, then released.

'Like that,' she breathed, smiling. 'That's amazing.'

Gently he thrust closer. 'Yeah,' He smiled back. 'Amazing.'

His hand splayed across her bottom, pushing her pelvis towards his until she grasped the rhythm. She wound her arms around him, holding tighter as his movement became faster, more fluid, stronger as he was sure of her pleasure.

'I knew it would be like this,' she murmured, almost mindless with bliss, wanting it never to end.

'Like what?' he asked raggedly.

'Perfect.'

He combed his fingers through her hair, his palm cupping the side of her face, holding her still so he could kiss the soul out of her. He broke it, looked into her eyes with those bottomless pools. She gazed back at him, their breathing mingling, meshing as one as their bodies did the same.

But she hadn't known it would be this intense. That she would feel this close to him emotionally as well as physically. She brushed a kiss across his shoulder so she could break that heart-stopping eye contact. When she glanced back at him he too had closed his eyes. She smiled when she saw how good it felt for him too. She ran her hands down his back, pressing him closer.

He surged harder, faster. 'Okay?' he muttered.

'Just don't stop.' Her eyes opened, wide, her vision suddenly acute as sensations shuddered through her. She ran her hands over him. Suddenly understanding that he was hers to touch now. That there was so much to explore and that until that moment she'd been doing exactly what he'd jeered he didn't want—just lying there.

So now she touched, now she hungered. She spread her legs wider, wrapping them round his hips to trap him in place while her hands swept south, searching out all his masculine secrets.

'Roxie,' he choked. He grabbed her wrists and pinned them above her head.

'I thought you didn't want someone just lying there,' she gasped. 'You don't want me to touch you?'

'Oh, I do. Later. But I won't last if you touch me like that now.'

She arched anyway, her body exposed and vulnerable to his. It struck her that at this one moment she was in his total possession. But she was also in his complete care. And he was taking such wicked, wonderful care as he bore down on her over and over and over until she convulsed beneath him, her body finally finding its long-sought completion.

His jaw was locked, his eyes burning as he watched

her, ensuring her physical fulfilment. She wasn't just fulfilled, she was all but delirious with ecstasy.

Gabe didn't think he'd ever breathe normally again—he seemed to be playing an impossible game of catch-up with his pulse. He'd always cared about whether his partner had a good time with him, but he'd wanted it to be better than good for her. He knew it would be unforgettable—it was her first time after all—but he'd wanted it to be unforgettable for so many more reasons than that.

So now he faced the uncomfortable truth. He hadn't had sex with her. He'd made love to her. Just a very little love—which was as new to him as it was to her. And in those moments in her arms, connected with her, he'd have done anything for her. A loss of free will he'd never before experienced. She might have lost her virginity, but he'd lost something too. Some part of himself was now locked within her and he wasn't sure he was going to get it back. A chunk of his heart he only now realised he'd actually had. He figured it served him right.

He also figured he could live without it. After all, he'd only just discovered it anyway so he could hardly miss it now. Besides, he was too busy wondering how soon until she'd be ready to take him again, or whether she was too tender—emotionally as well as physically. He frowned. He really had to keep a lid on this somehow. Stop her from wanting too much other than the physical. Because he really wanted her to want some more physical. But how the hell did he balance it?

'You like sleeping in here?' She broke the silence lazily, stretching out on the bed beside him with a little moan that made his blood rush all over his beat body.

'It has the best view,' he answered without thinking. From his bed he could see straight out that one window across the floor—its view encompassed the garage, and that other window in the flat above.

'Have you been watching me?'

He could hear her smile. 'I've seen you in the garden a few times. But you know that.'

She rolled towards him, then he felt her smile kiss his shoulder. 'Yes, I know.'

He cleared his throat. Hoped she didn't think he'd been watching because he was besotted or anything. She wore the skimpiest shorts and vest-top combos ever—of course he looked. Any man would. Oh, man, how did he handle this now?

But she rose up onto her elbow and peered, reading his expression. 'Stop looking so worried, Gabe. I'm not going to fall in love with you,' she scoffed.

He stared at her. Since when was he that much of an open book?

She smiled—easy and amused and happy. 'I told you last night, I'm not going to want anything more from you.'

Good. 'Cos he didn't want that either—right? Only now, contrarily, he did want more. More like right now.

She leaned right over him, brushing her hair back behind her ears, her blue eyes looking earnestly into his. 'You know I'm not interested in a relationship, right? As fantastic as that was and as gorgeous as you are.'

He managed to nod. She'd just spoken words he'd said so often in the past.

'This was just a one-off.'

A one-off? *Really?* 'Sure.' He faked a grin.

She smiled wider, clearly genuine. 'Great. The minute the whistle blows on the final this season, I'm out of here. I'm booking my ticket as soon as the bank lets me.'

'You really are?' He'd been wondering about those plans of hers.

'Yeah, so don't renege on our rental agreement, will you? I need the money to pay for it.'

He shook his head slowly. 'I won't.'

'Great.' She slipped out of the bed with a way too energetic wriggle. 'I really appreciate your effort today. Thank you.'

So that was it? He'd helped her lose the virgin tag and she'd appreciated his effort in doing so? It was like getting a report card from school. His *effort*? Where was the bloody award of excellence? Didn't she know out-of-this-world sex when she had it?

His heart seized. One day she'd learn that that hadn't been average sex. He tried to stop that direction of his thoughts—because the idea of her being in some other guy's arms, of some guy not doing it good enough for her? Oh, now he was beyond grumpy. His freaking *effort*? The more he thought about it, the more it stung. The more he wanted to roar.

She glanced back, brows lifting at his silence and her skin suddenly washed beet red. 'Oh, I'm sorry about…'

He glanced down, then quickly covered the stained sheet. 'Forget it.'

But it was as if she had already. Oh, the irony. *He* was the one feeling like the emotional innocent. As if sleeping with someone made you feel something more than mere physical fun. Intimacy. Caring. As if it all should have mattered so much more to her than to warrant a good *effort* sticker. Damn. He couldn't be feeling used because he'd known exactly what she'd wanted. It was what he'd wanted too. Those desires had finally converged and now it was finished. Right? Sure.

She was slipping her dress over her head, not bothering with either bra or knickers. He was trying hard not to get turned on by that. And failing.

'You're going?' he asked.

It was obvious doofus. Did he have to make his un-expectedly massive disappointment just as obvious?

'Yeah, you've got to get to work later, right?' she answered breezily. 'And I need to do some work in the garden.'

She wanted to *garden* over spending more time in bed with him? That was a kicker. To his bemusement she walked out of the room. A minute later he sat up, watching out of the window as she took the trail through the tomato plants to the rickety flight of stairs along the garage's rear wall. He peeled his aching body from the bed. No way was he going to spend the afternoon watching her shaking it in the garden.

He drove to the beach, pushed through the physical exhaustion to run a mile along the shore. The entire time he thought of nothing but her—wanting nothing more than to be snuggled with her and sound asleep. And the doubts started, the worries. He found himself walking instead of running and chewing on his blasted thumb-nail. Because now he wanted to know for sure that she really was okay. Maybe she was back at that house feeling all anxious. Maybe her casual goodbye this morning had been all façade—an attempt at sophistication like her hair and her lip gloss and her damn fake chicken fillets. Maybe she was up in that horrendous bedsit of hers bawling her eyes out and about to go scary emo on him.

Oh, hell. Hadn't he better go make sure she was okay?

CHAPTER EIGHT

ROXIE breathed deep and smiled—to keep her good vibe
even. She knew all about laughter therapy—that if you
were down, even just putting on a smile lifted your mood
up a few notches. Not that she was down, of course.
No way could any kind of sadness sink her now—after
all, she'd gotten what she'd wanted. The most incredible experience. Now it was finished and that was fine.
She wasn't going to fall for him. No, if anything, what
she felt was *gratitude*. He'd given everything she'd ever
wanted—fun, courtesy, ecstasy. She knew it all now.
And sure, she could see why some girls went crazy
for the guy who gave that kind of absolute joy. But *she*
wasn't going to lose it.

Having said that, it had to be a one-time-only. Once
definitely had to be enough. And honestly it was—she
was so exhausted she could hardly move. No way could
she manage a replay anyway. She stepped out of her hot
shower and pulled on a fresh tee shirt. She curled up on
her camp bed, pulling her pillow under her cheek, and
relaxed as tiredness overwhelmed her. Tiredness and satisfaction—that tiny hint of forlorn determinedly forgotten. She forced herself to focus on upcoming European
destinations. But as she drifted to sleep it was him she
dwelt on—his smile, his tease, the comfort of his arms.

'Roxie.'

She moaned and rolled over. Dreaming of him, of the way he'd groaned her name as he'd surged inside her.

'Roxie!'

Okay, he didn't usually shout like that—not in her dreams.

'Open the damn door!'

She pushed her hair back from her face, blinking rapidly to try to bring her brain back from the sensually charged sleep state it had been in the last couple of hours. She stumbled to the door.

'Is everything okay?' he asked as soon as she opened it. 'I've been knocking for ages.'

He was wearing shorts and a fitted tee and had clearly been out running. She could hardly drag her eyes up to his face. Her dreams broke their boundaries, sending images—some real memories, some utter fantasies— scrolling through her mind. All involving him *without* those shorts.

'Sure,' she mumbled. 'I was sleeping.'

She looked into his face; his eyes were focused on her and a heavy frown had obliterated his earlier satisfied expression.

'Is there something you wanted?' Her question trailed off. There was something going on with her body; she could feel it priming again. She breathed in, her senses filled with nothing but him—his height, his scent, the harsh sound from his throat as he'd hit his release. She squeezed her pelvic floor muscles to try to stop the melting sensation. It only made it worse.

'You were really asleep?' The dark centres of his eyes swelled.

'Sure,' she said, starting to laugh. 'I was tired—it was a late night.'

'You've really been asleep this whole time?'

'Well, I had a shower...' She stepped back as he pushed past her and hunched down by her bar fridge. He drew out the bottle with the V marked on it.

'Why didn't you come back here this morning and have a champagne brunch to celebrate your new non-virgin status?' Now he had the smile on—that rakish one.

'I was waiting to have it with dinner tonight.' Truthfully she'd forgotten about it. 'But maybe I'll open it now.'

Her mouth was so dry, the drink would help. She held out her hand for it.

'You know, you don't deserve it yet.' He stood and held the bottle out of reach.

'I'm no longer a virgin, Gabe, as I do believe you know.' She couldn't resist the husky reminder.

'I disagree.'

She gaped at him. 'Tell me I didn't dream it.'

'No,' he chuckled. 'But there are so many ways in which you are still a virgin. So you've had a little vanilla sex. Missionary style. Shouldn't you be trying out all the options?'

'What other options did you have in mind?' Fascinated, she moved closer.

'Strikes me you have an interesting mind of your own, Roxie. What have you thought about?'

The heat flushed through her body. She didn't know if she should answer that.

His eyes gleamed and he leaned closer so they were almost, almost touching. 'Don't try and tell me you haven't thought about a few things.'

Okay, so it was going to be more than once. He was

right, there was a lot she'd yet to experience. And she wanted to try it all with him.

'You might regret asking this,' she breathed. 'Because the whole time you've been out exercising, I've been sleeping. You might not have the stamina to keep up with me.'

'Somehow I think I'll cope.' He swallowed. 'So you want to investigate this further?'

'There isn't a "this" between us.' There couldn't be. She was *free*; that was the whole point.

'No, I meant *your* sensual nature. Don't you want to explore that some more?'

Oh, she did. She really, really did. With him.

'And which was more fun?' he asked. 'The fantasy or the reality?'

'This is all a kind of fantasy,' she said honestly.

'Okay.' He nodded. 'But while you can pretend your hands are mine, there are a couple of things you need me in the flesh for, right?'

Oh, yeah, she needed that flesh. Badly. She moved another step towards him. 'I'm going away at the end of the season.'

'We'll be done before then anyway. Easy, right?'

'Really easy.' Oh, just so easy, so nothing more.

He walked closer to meet her. 'So what other ways, Roxie? Standing, sitting, doggy, on a table, in the shower?'

'Reverse cowgirl.'

'What?'

'Reverse cowgirl.'

A distracted look crossed his face. 'Sure, that too.'

'Shall we draw up a list?' 'Cos she had a large number of ideas in her head already.

'By all means write up a list. So long as I can add to

it. Hold this.' He thrust the bottle into her hands then swooped and picked her up. She giggled as he strode out of her little flat, down the stairs, not stopping 'til he'd barged into his own bedroom. 'And there has to be some room for spontaneity.'

It seemed sometimes spontaneity involved a champagne shower.

When Gabe woke the next morning—alone—he spotted a single sheet of paper Blu-Tacked to the wall. On it was a neatly written list. Bullet points and everything. He both blushed and chuckled as he read it. Seemed Roxie had a flair for fantasy—or had some tantric sex manual stashed somewhere, because even he wasn't sure what she meant by some of those suggestions. But, man, was he happy at the thought of finding out. On the negative side, it meant his day at the stadium dragged unbelievably slowly.

She was in the garden when he got home. But he thought he should try to hold off for at least five minutes, to prove to himself that he could more than anything. He made a show of looking at the ridiculously huge, abundant green garden, trying not to explode at the way she stroked his chest in explicit welcome.

'You have enough vegetables here to feed the team three times over,' he said.

Roxie gave the beds a fleeting glance, really not caring about them that second. 'There's not that many. I can eat a lot.'

She saw him glance over her sceptically.

'When you only eat plant, you eat a lot of plant,' she pointed out.

'Is now a bad time to admit that I come from generations of farmers? With several farms. Beef, dairy and sheep.' He even looked sheepish as he said it.

'Meat central, huh?' She shrugged. 'I guess we do live in New Zealand—fifty sheep per person and all that.'

He chuckled. 'I don't think it's that many. And I didn't follow the plan, did medicine instead. That make me more acceptable?'

Oh, the man was so much more than acceptable. But she couldn't afford to admit that, and his ego didn't need fattening. 'Marginally.'

'Marginally?' He looked affronted. 'Doctors save lives.'

She shot him a teasing look. 'How many lives do you save, Gabe? You're a sports specialist.'

'I save a lot of lives, actually,' he said, quite seriously. 'Think about it. You're a dancer, right? So you know something of what it's like to spend every minute of every day training for that one goal. Of making all kinds of sacrifices to try to meet that goal. So what happens if you get an injury and it threatens to snatch it all from you in a second? Don't you want a doctor on hand then?'

Okay, so she could give him that. 'Didn't your family want you to do medicine?'

He shook his head. 'The firstborn son must grow up and take over the farming empire. It's written in stone. That archaic belief in primogeniture.'

Oh, her curiosity was piqued. 'You're the firstborn son?'

'Uh-huh.'

'Of how many?' Yes, totally curious now.

'Just my sister and me.'

She wondered what his sister was like. What his parents were like. Wondered a ton of things she had no real business wondering. That didn't stop her asking. 'And you didn't want to farm?'

'Do I look like a farmer?' he joked.

In his on-trend jeans, tee and trainers, she had to admit he didn't. 'Is it too much hard work for you?' She couldn't resist teasing him some more.

'It's too far out in the country for me.' He matched her tone. 'I love to visit but don't want to live there. I like the city.'

'Because you like to be near a high-density female population? I'm guessing there aren't nearly enough women in the countryside for you.'

'Exactly.' He grinned. 'I need the variety. But of course the family doesn't approve.'

'Of all the women or the lack of farming interest?'

'Both.' He winked. 'I'm a wayward terror.'

Roxie shook her head. The guy was over-egging it. 'You're not that much of a terror. Look how hard I had to push you to take me to bed. I don't think there's much substance to your rogue reputation.'

'Ah, but that was because I was trying to reform my wicked ways.'

He had her absolute attention now. 'And why was that?' She watched him close, curious to see if he'd answer.

It seemed he'd decided to give the nearest tomato plant a thorough inspection, bending down to see if the cherry-sized reds were ripe for picking. 'I get the feeling you might already know about it.'

'Diana,' she confirmed softly.

He snapped off the first fruit. 'What did they tell you?'

Roxie decided to be completely honest. 'I'm a new dancer for the Blades—first thing they did was warn me away from you.'

He swivelled to look at her, his brows impossibly high. 'But you ignored them.'

She shrugged. 'I'm not as vulnerable as it seemed she'd been.'

He looked uncomfortable and turned back to the plant, started a picking frenzy. 'She wasn't exactly healthy, no. I didn't know that when we started dating.'

'So what happened?' She moved up beside him and held her hands out so he could put his growing collection of tomatoes into them.

He avoided answering by popping a tomato into his mouth—putting one into her mouth too. She ignored the sweet sensation that flared deep inside—not just from the sun-warmed sweet fruit, but from the feeling of intimacy in him having fed it to her. Determinedly she kept looking at him—her brows raised as she waited for him to spill it.

'Okay, we dated,' he said after finally swallowing. 'Just normal dating—which for me is usually fairly short term, right?' He gave her a keen look.

Roxie grinned. 'Yeah, but I'm guessing she didn't take that on board?'

'I ended it—way soon even for me. But she'd got it into her head that we were supposed to be soul mates or something. It got very awkward and she became increasingly hysterical. She was on my doorstep, she'd turn up at events I attended. I went away with the team and when I got back she'd actually moved into my apartment. All her stuff, everything, and was acting like... I don't know. It had gone from awkward to ugly to dangerous. She threatened all kinds of things. I called a friend who's a psych. We called her family. But it was bad, it was really bad. And after that I decided to take a break from dating altogether.'

Which was why he'd been so grumpy? Because a dating break wasn't his natural style. Yeah, she knew he wasn't entirely the heartless playboy he had the rep for, but he did like to have some fun. She moved to put the tomatoes on the outdoor table, pleased he'd been honest enough to tell her about it. She liked that he'd been bothered someone had been hurt—even if it wasn't really his fault. She guessed Diana had other issues too, it had all just come to a head with Gabe. Poor guy, she didn't think he'd deserved to put himself into penance for months like that. She smiled at him as he followed her and added yet more tomatoes to the collection.

'You do know I'm not going to go stalker on you, right?' He had nothing to fear from her.

'Yes, I do know that.' He broke eye contact—staring across the garden instead.

There was an oddly fixed silence.

'So what does your family think of your career now?' she asked, just to break it. 'You *can't* be a disappointment, you're a doctor.'

That brought a slight smile back. 'Even just a sports doctor?'

'You know I was only teasing.' She'd seen for herself how highly regarded he was at the stadium—the team totally relied on him.

'Yeah, well. You're not the first to make an issue of it. No, my dad didn't want me to do medicine. You're looking at Andrew G. Hollingsworth the sixth and the first to betray the family and walk off the land.'

'Andrew?' That threw her—Andrew didn't suit him at all.

'Andrew Gabriel,' he explained. 'Gabe.'

Gabe was so much better, with those heavenly connotations and all—she knew just *how* heavenly he felt. 'Did that go down badly too?'

'Unbelievably,' he answered briefly, picking up another tomato and munching on it.

'Were you written out of the will?' she joked.

'For a while.' He nodded and answered out of the side of his mouth. 'But I wasn't going to back down. I'm not having my entire life dictated by other people's expectations.'

Freedom was important to him too, huh? Roxie walked over to the tap at the back of the garage so she could rinse the plant scent from her fingers. 'So how did you break free?' she asked when he came beside her, waiting for his turn under the tap.

'I ran away to the city, which wasn't the smartest move, but at the time it was all I had. It's not that easy to go against the wishes of your whole family when you've been groomed from the moment of conception—"one day this will all be yours, your responsibility" blah, blah, blah.'

'Did they come after you?'

He shook his head. 'I was seventeen and we didn't communicate for over a year.'

'That's awful.' How could they do that to a son who was everything any sane parent would want? Not just fit and healthy but bright and super successful and *everything*.

'It wasn't so bad.' He smiled when he saw the expression on her face. 'I had friends. Studied, played rugby. And I kept in touch with my sister because she was at boarding school. Honestly, the things I missed most were the lambs I'd reared and my dog.'

'You had lambs?' She was momentarily diverted by that cute mental image. Was even more diverted when

Gabe cupped his hand under the still running water and then sipped from it.

'Took the orphans in each season,' he explained after he swallowed.

She refused to ask if they'd had them for Christmas dinner.

'No, I didn't eat them, they were pets.' He read her mind as he turned off the tap. 'Anyway, Mum got steadily madder and madder with Dad. In the end they had a massive blow-up.'

'Hooray for your mum.' Roxie really hoped she'd withheld conjugal rights and everything.

'She insisted Dad and I get together. I told him what I was going to do with my life and if he wanted to be a part of it, he had to accept it.'

Take-no-prisoners Gabe—the man was tough—but then it seemed he'd had to be to get free. That was something she could understand. And admire. 'And he did?'

'Eventually.'

Wow. Roxie knew how conflict within families could change people. That lack of support must have affected him—and his ability to trust.

'What about your sister? Did your dad have some grand plan for her too?'

'Well, here's the ironic thing—she loves farming. But she's a girl.'

'Don't tell me girls can't be farmers?' Roxie caught on quick.

'Never. No such thing as a lady farmer,' he joked.

Roxie felt as bad for his sister as she had for Gabe. It was only circumstance that had held Roxie back from doing all she'd wanted to—her grandparents' health, but they'd been supportive and caring in every other way possible. They'd always believed in her, in fact she'd downplayed her disappointment at having to stop dance lessons so as not to distress them. 'That's just crazy.'

'Isn't it?' He wiped his mouth with the back of his hand. A couple of drops still remained just below his lip. Roxie wanted to kiss them away.

'So there was the guy wanting an heir to take over the place and he had one chomping at the bit and he couldn't even see it,' Gabe continued. 'I told her to get out of there and do her thing and I'd back her up.'

Roxie felt a bit sorry for his mum now. Must have been hard having both her kids feeling as if they had to *escape*.

'My sister, the natural-born farmer, did an agriculture degree. Won top honours of her year. You should have seen Dad at her graduation. So now they're working together on the farms and everybody's happy and the big bust-up is all in the past and done with.'

Was it? Roxie heard that slight edge in his voice and knew she was right—wounds like that left scars. 'But it was worth it?'

'No one was telling me what to do with my own life. I won't be hemmed in,' he said firmly. 'And I guess it's why I like working with the team, helping those guys achieve their ambition. Everybody should be free to chase their own dreams.' He shot her a suddenly embarrassed look. 'That's really cheesy, isn't it?'

'No, it's not,' she said honestly. 'Your sister must have liked having you in her corner.'

He laughed—full of self-mockery. 'I was totally selfish. I just wanted to stay at med school and live it up in town. It was in my interest to see them sort it out. And now they can finally cope with my job because I get them VIP tickets to all the big games.'

'But I'm guessing they could afford to buy their own tickets if they really wanted to, right?'

His expression completely sobered. 'Yeah, there's a lot of money. And I'm back in the will—am a shareholder in the estate. The Hollingsworth clan has finally landed in the twenty-first century. That's the reason women say yes to me—they know the value of my surname.'

Roxie froze for a split second and then roared with laughter.

'Gabe,' she gasped when she could, wiping a tear from her eye and breathing deep to ease the stitch in her tummy. 'That's *not* why they say yes.' She smiled up at him as her amusement threatened an uncontrollable return.

But he wasn't smiling back. He was just watching her, a slight knot between his brows, as if some thought up in his brain was uncomfortable. His gaze dropped, zoomed in on her mouth. She knew exactly what he was thinking now. Only instead of acting on that urge, he turned away. The frown crease deepening on his forehead. Disappointed, she watched him walk towards the house. What, were they not going to tick an item off her list tonight? Well, that was disappointing—she'd been hanging out for it all day at work. Had she offended him somehow? How did she bring back the play in him?

'Want to know one of my favourite things?' she called, suddenly hit by inspiration.

He wheeled on the spot.

'Wait there, I've got to get it.' She raced up to her flat, fearing he'd go into the Treehouse and leave her all hot and bothered and alone.

But instead he followed her up the stairs. 'Let me guess, champagne?'

'No, this.' She turned and brandished the bottle.

Maple syrup. Gabe looked at the label and whipped his head up to read her face. 'Oh, my.' Goosebumps smothered his skin. 'What are you planning to—?'

'You know already.' She smiled that totally audacious smile.

He adjusted his stance because his body was rioting. And he just gave in to it. Anticipation blasted away the sting he'd felt from her saying she wasn't going to go stalker on him. Why it had kicked he didn't know, and why would he fight the vision of seduction in front of him now? He didn't have to fight it any more; they wanted the same thing—nothing but fun frolics for a few weeks...

She paused from unscrewing the lid of the bottle. The amusement flashing in her eyes undermined the innocence of her smile. 'I thought you liked spontaneity.'

'I do,' he muttered, suddenly breathless.

Mere minutes later Gabe was flat on his back on the floor and wondering if he was about to have a cardiac arrest. It sure as hell felt like it. 'Where did you learn to do that?' he gasped.

'A magazine, where else?' She sat up, her hair tumbling down her back, her cheeks rosy, her lips still slick from the syrup she'd licked and sucked from him. 'The article said it would send you cross-eyed. Did it work?'

Well, his head was spinning and his heart reeling. And seeing her look like the ultimate hedonistic nymph, he had to screw his eyes shut tight again.

'Long live women's magazines,' he muttered fervently. Another realisation dawned as he absorbed her words. 'Was that your first time?'

'Mmm hmm.' She sounded very pleased with herself.

He sat up in a hurry, fully focused on her now. She'd never gone down on a guy before and she did it like that?

Such a natural it was unnatural. As she licked her lips he took her by surprise and pushed her back, settling his body over hers so she couldn't escape. It truly was sick how much he liked having her beneath him. He tugged down her shorts, then slid so his face was where they'd just been. His hands held her wrists to her sides and he looked up her belly and between her breasts to her very wide blue eyes.

'What about the situation in reverse?' He brushed the lightest kiss across her upper thigh. 'Has anyone ever done this to you?'

It took her a moment, then she slowly shook her head.

His instincts burned. 'I thought you said your virginity was a mere technicality, that you were no novice. But you haven't even had oral sex?' Hell, that was the thing lots of teen technical virgins did, right? How they got off without going all the way.

Her flush deepened. She shook her head again.

He paused, too late to go back now—and now he needed to know it all. 'So why me?'

'You know what you're doing?' she answered in a small, uncertain voice.

He figured that was a partially honest answer, he looked at her steadily waiting for more. Hoping there *was* more.

'And I think you're very nice,' she added in an even smaller voice. 'I'm very attracted to you and I trust you to do what I need you to do. *All* I need you to do.'

He watched more closely. 'Why do you trust me?'

'Because you already have.'

Done what she'd needed? Shown her a good time in bed and let her keep it so casual they didn't even spend ten minutes together out of the sack?

All of a sudden it wasn't enough.

'Tell me about the boyfriend,' he prompted. 'Did he even exist?'

'Yes, he did,' she answered. 'We dated for a few months.'

'A few *months*?' Gabe was amazed. How on earth had she stopped herself from shagging him? She was insatiable. And curious. And determined. 'He'd taken a celibacy vow?'

'No.' She pulled a wrist free and mock-slapped him. 'There just wasn't the opportunity.'

'You could have found an opportunity.' She so could have.

'I didn't want to.'

And that was the answer he'd been seeking. Yeah, contrary to his keep-it-casual intentions, it pleased him no end that she was hot for him in a way she'd not been hot for anyone else. But he wanted her to appreciate some of his other skills too. Oh, he did not want this to become some sordid, nothing but sex-travaganza. There were other things he wanted—like a little more of her respect, to soothe that little chunk she'd taken out of him.

Yeah, his ex-*non*-accidental-virgin was about to get a little more than she'd bargained for.

CHAPTER NINE

ROXIE sent him packing, using her minuscule shower as her excuse. Truly, she'd just needed to breathe. No, she hadn't slept with Jake, because Jake had never turned her on to the point that she was a writhing, panting, incoherent mess of sensation—as she'd just been on her cold, hard floor. She couldn't believe she'd let Gabe do all that boundary-breaking intimate stuff. Or that she'd done it to him first. Or that she'd liked it so much she was hot again already. But she was hanging onto this new-found audacity. This was fun—so long as she could keep it all within her control. And her flight instinct told her that meant maintaining some distance.

She pulled on some clothes and realised she was hungry for food. She snuck down the stairs to get some greens to add to her dinner. He was on the deck, sticking his knife into a giant steak. Masses of potatoes encircled it. He was clearly both carbo-loading and replenishing muscle. That would be useful—later—when she was ready to deal with him some more.

Gabe swallowed a smile at the dirty look she gave his dinner, but she said nothing. It amused him that she'd had no idea of what his name meant. It really was the reason so many of those dancers had set their sights on him rather than a rugby boy. His name—and family—was synonymous with farming wealth. So she was wrong about the sex-stud thing, and there were a few more things it wouldn't do her any harm to learn about him. Except she didn't seem to be interested in doing anything with him but the salacious. But he planned to change that.

'Why not sit here to have your dinner?' he asked casually. 'You can't sit at your table up there with all that furniture and crap crammed around it. Have it down here. I promise I won't bite.' It was more a dare than an invitation.

She didn't answer immediately. Interesting how at ease she was with him when they were physical, and how uncomfortable she was at the thought of spending more simple, sex-free time with him. Was she actually *shy*? That didn't make sense when she'd been nothing but smart'n'sassy and strong from word go. Assertive beyond belief. He thought about it more carefully—about how she'd hung on the edge of the group of dancers at the after-practice drinks, how she'd hidden in the dark instead of confiding to anyone about her nerves before the game, how she lived behind a giant hedge no one would be mad enough to fight through. Suddenly, the idea of her being shy made more sense than anything.

'I'm nearly done anyway.' He tried to make it easier for her.

She shrugged. 'I have to get the rest of it.'

'So go get it,' he said, as if he didn't care. Wished he didn't care half as much as he feared he could.

Three minutes later she perched on the edge of the seat opposite his, her plate full of rabbit food. No wonder she was so slim. He kept the conversation light. Stadium-related stories mostly, until she warmed up and laughed. Until she started talking back. Topping some of his tales with mad-old-lady shopping tales of her own. Turned out her day job was at the gift store at the corner shops, a store no one from their generation would ordinarily enter. He couldn't understand why she worked there—if she wanted to work in retail, why not some high-dollar fashion place? She had the physique to wear those expensive, slinky numbers and have all the customers desperate to look just like her. That was just one of several things he was biding his time to ask her. But for now, he just talked—nothing too personal or too heavy, but enough to entertain and keep her there until it was late and dark and the bedroom beckoned.

In his big bed in her old room, Roxie stretched. It really was time for her to slope across the garden and curl up on her own hard, narrow stretcher that reminded her of reality. But Gabe's big arms encircled her. He lifted her, repositioning her so his chest was her pillow, his hand worked through her hair and he rubbed the base of her skull. She let it happen—it felt too good to pull from. Just a few more minutes. No harm would come from that little bit of closeness—right?

'Why haven't you gone travelling sooner?' he asked lazily.

'I needed to get this place ready.' The repairs after the earthquake had cost money that had taken her a long time to earn.

'But you've never got round to trimming the hedge?'

She laughed gently. 'No. At first it was just because I was too busy to get to it. Then I noticed it kept people out. I liked that, keeping my privacy.'

She felt the vibrations in his chest as he chuckled with her—it made for a wonderfully relaxing kind of massage.

'So what are you going to do once the champagne runs out?' he asked. 'Is there a new list or are you just going to travel indefinitely?'

She breathed in deep and sighed as she answered. 'There's a new list. I'll have to find some champagne over there.' There had to be a new list—her life would just be beginning over there, right? The start of her freedom.

'Where's there? What's first on the list?'

She smiled up at the ceiling as she thought about it. 'You're going to think it's lame.'

'No, I won't.'

Oh, he so would. 'I want to go to the ballet in London.'

'The ballet? That's number one?'

She chuckled. Yeah, he wasn't that wowed. 'Don't knock it. I studied for thirteen years, started when I was three. I've been dreaming of going there for ever.'

'If you loved it so much why'd you give up?' He firmly slid his hand down her back, pulled her lax body even closer. 'You couldn't afford classes any more?'

'Actually my teacher offered to waive the fees, but it was the time more than the money. There were other things I had to do.' Her grandmother had just had the stroke; her grandfather had needed help caring for her.

There was a small silence, as if he was waiting for her to say something more. Which she didn't.

'So the ballet—in London?' he finally prompted— with a distinct lack of enthusiasm.

'Yeah, the Royal Ballet at Covent Garden. To see one of the classics. Not your thing, huh?'

She felt his laughter again. 'All those blokes leaping about in tights and no one saying anything? Nah.'

She nudged his thigh with her knee and teased. 'I knew you were going to comment about the tights. Why do guys always feel so threatened by them? Hell, the rugby players wear almost as little—their shirts are skin-tight.'

'Well, it's not just the men I'm not so keen on. All the girls are bony. They've got no shape, no boobs, where's the attraction in watching them? They're not exactly sexy.'

Roxie sat up indignantly and twisted to see his face in the moonlight. 'You don't like skinny dancers? Then why have you dated so many?'

'Not *that* many.' He went on instant defence. 'And I didn't date them because they were dancers—it was just that they were who I happened to meet.'

Oh, so it was a circumstantial thing, not that dancer girls were his 'type'? She was fairly surprised—and surprisingly miffed. 'So you don't like the ballerina body?'

He paused, a grin suddenly flaring, and he reached up to pull her back to him. 'I think you know how I feel about your body, Roxie.'

Yeah, that wasn't good enough. She resisted his tug closer and waited, fingers tapping on his chest.

'It's not just beautiful.' His grin widened as he unashamedly back-pedalled. 'It's the way you move. You know what you're doing, but it's like its unconscious at the same time. Total natural grace and not like anyone else I've met. Ever.'

'You need to keep the compliments coming because I'm still feeling insecure about the no-boobs bit.'

He laughed harder; she felt his body harden too. 'You do great in that department.'

'With my booster bra.'

'I like them best with no bra, as well you know.' He slid a broad, warm palm up over her stomach, towards her ribcage, as if to prove it. 'In fact, you'd be fantastic at burlesque,' he teased. 'You know, with those nipple tassles?'

'Oh, you would know all about nipple tassles,' she huffed, twisting away to leave him.

Except he grabbed her so she couldn't, pulling her back and rolling so he had her pinned, oh, so pleasurably. Admittedly she didn't put up too much of a fight.

'You want to dance full time?' His mouth hovered above where he wanted those damn tassles.

'When I was a kid I did,' she answered breathlessly, getting distracted by what his tongue was now doing. 'Reality is, not many people can make a viable living as a dancer. Even if you can it's not for long—you're arthritic at thirty. That's why scoring the gig with the Blades was such a thrill—even for just a short time I'm a pro.'

'You shouldn't settle for only a short time. Why not go the whole hog?'

'It's too late for classical,' she moaned. 'I'm over the hill already.'

His grunt of laughter was muffled against her breast and his fingers teased further south. 'There are other forms of dance.'

'I'm sorry to disappoint you, Gabe,' she panted. 'But I don't think burlesque is for me.'

He flexed, teasing her more exquisitely. 'You could teach or make up the Blades' routines or have your own shop—you like retail, right? Why not dance gear?'

She actually quite liked that idea. Having a retail space with a studio above it to teach or something. 'I used to love going to the ballet shop and looking at the costumes.'

'You love a costume, Roxie?'

'You bet I do.' Yeah, she had a soft spot for sequins and Lycra.

'Well, I really think you should try the tassles.' His voice deepened with laughter as she wriggled against him. 'Not many women could, you know. That's a real compliment.'

She muttered an adjective so colourful he instantly reared up and took her hard.

She had no idea how much later it was when he lifted her back with her head resting on his shoulder. All she knew was that she was utterly relaxed and bone-deep exhausted. She closed her eyes, her own breathing falling into sync with the deep, regular rise and fall of his broad chest. So very vaguely the thought pinched—she really *ought* to go back to her own place. But she was so tired. And so warm. And she'd never been held like this by anyone…so finding the energy to leave this haven was going to take a few minutes.

'You miss your grandparents?' he asked softly, gently rubbing her shoulders with the tips of his fingers in light, slow circles.

The question was so out of the blue she answered without even thinking about it. 'Every day.'

'And you've never tried to track down your father?'

That brought her back from the brink of sleep, but his fingers kept up the rhythmic kneading. She sighed—so damn tired and, while he was soothing, he was also holding her in an embrace she'd have to push hard to break free of. So she just gave in and told the truth. 'No information to go on,' she murmured, her eyelids drooping.

Time drifted and she floated deeper into the warm, velvety darkness. She felt so comfortable it had to be a dream…and, yeah, she wasn't sure if she really heard the next question or not.

'You really know nothing?'

'There's no one left to ask, nothing in the papers.' As she slipped into that half-sleep state the futility was the last thing she remembered. 'Day after I was born she left for the UK and never came back. Asked Grandies a couple of times but I didn't want to hurt them. *They* were my parents.' For years she hadn't pushed it because she'd known it had distressed them. 'They always told me the same story—Mum was young and hadn't wanted to be tied down. She'd had an affair but didn't want an abortion, but didn't want to be an involved mother either. They wanted to keep me in the family. So I never went off the straight and narrow 'cos I knew how much Mum's mess hurt them. And me. So I was a total good-girl. Almost. Dated Jake. But did nothing that would devastate them if they ever found out. But he didn't understand why I never went out for a drink or clubbing. Never stayed out late, never swore. Never did any normal teenage rebel things. Grandma got sick and needed me.'

She burrowed deeper into the warmth, seeking to escape. But her mind skittered through the memories relentlessly. She'd grown up in ways her more experienced friends hadn't. And those friends had been too busy with their own parties and teen issues to deal with her own sombre ones. She'd learned not to talk about her life at home—too much of a downer. Too unrelatable. And it was easier not to talk because she could hardly bear to face it herself—the inevitable loss that had loomed. First one, then the other. Until she was left alone.

'They were older parents when they had Mum and she'd been headstrong and wilful. I couldn't do that to them too. But now they're gone and I can do whatever.' She was answerable only to herself—free. While she didn't resent a minute of her life up to now, now was *her* time. Maybe that was what she'd inherited from her mother—that need never to be tied down. 'I always wonder why she didn't want me. Why did she leave me and go overseas if there wasn't something that hurt her to even look at me?'

The high-pitched, harsh question woke Roxie. She swallowed and felt the roughness in her throat. That was when she realised it had been *her* talking. And she was being held in a tighter-than-tight embrace. She was awake—and, even worse, *he* was awake and she'd just been spilling all this stuff *aloud* and she'd never said it to *anyone*. Eyes flashing wide open, she froze in position, her skin goosebumping, her heart hardening. Oh, hell, this had been dumb. She couldn't let the happy-after-orgasm hormones confuse her into thinking there was *intimacy* here. And she most certainly didn't want him feeling sorry for her or thinking she was some kind of stuffed-up, incapable, needy person. She was totally capable—and totally embarrassed. All her internal alarms clanged—way past time to go back to the garage and get this non-relationship back to its clearly delineated fun-only status.

But she had to make her exit smooth and unpanicked-like. As if she hadn't just confessed some of her innermost turmoil or anything. She pressed a couple of kisses to his shoulder and slipped out when his hold eased the tiniest amount. Then desperately tried to think of something completely safe to discuss. Glancing out of the window at the dark shadows of the garden outside, she landed on it.

'Do you mind if I use your kitchen to make some things with the tomato glut?' she asked as she felt on the floor for her clothes. Because the last thing she wanted him thinking was that she was trying to move in on his space by stealth. 'I'll do it when you're at work.'

'Course I don't mind.' Gabe minded that she felt she had to ask. Damn, for a few minutes there he'd thought he'd been busting through her reserve—which was more prickly than that damn hedge outside. But obviously not, given she was now asking permission for the simplest of things, given she'd suddenly stiffened as if she hadn't re-alised what she'd been saying, given her voice had gone from sleepy-slurred to shrill and given how quickly she was escaping from him now.

'It's just that my kitchen's not big enough.'

He made a deal of pulling up the duvet to stop himself glaring at her. She even felt as if she had to explain?

'You don't *have* a kitchen.' He couldn't resist the dig. She had a gas ring, a microwave and a fridge half full of champagne.

She merely smiled and waved as she left.

Gabe slumped lower in bed and tried to kick away the disappointment and dissatisfaction. He had absolutely no fear of Roxie walking in and taking over his home à la Diana. If it weren't for the scent of her lingering on his sheets, there'd be no clue that she'd been there with him at all. And now, not for the first time, he wished she'd stay in the house with him. He'd even had the mad thought of doing something to the garage so she'd *have* to move in. Because those rickety stairs made him shudder. So did her isolation.

When he got back from the stadium one afternoon a few days later, it was to find the windows open and the relentless beat of dance music vibrating through the hedge. He rubbed his knuckles over his chest—first time in his life he felt his heart literally lift.

The Knights had had another home game. Roxie had

danced, he'd doctored. They hadn't attended the after-match celebrations. They'd gone home and had one of their own. Every night since they'd had separate dinners together on the deck. He'd engaged her in more—easy—conversation, even managed to get her to watch movies with him. The first night he'd had to surrender to her choice of those awful dance flicks—but it had been worth it when she gave him her own demo of the theme moves. Now they alternated—dance flicks, then thrillers. Gabe was pleased about it. He didn't like to think of her being in that tiny studio alone—no reason why they couldn't hang out together a bit. Still easy, right?

She was in his kitchen—looking more Roxanna than Roxie with her hair pulled back into a plait, not a skerrick of make-up, and swamped in an apron. But then she saw him—and there was a flutter of eyelids and a flash of blue that was pure Roxie.

He strode over—it smelt good. 'Let me try it.'

She pulled a spoon from the drawer and dipped it into the oversized pot that scarily resembled a witch's cauldron.

'Mmm.' Impossibly, it tasted better than it smelt.

'No salt, no egg, no dairy, no oil, no gluten, no meat—'

'No fun,' he inserted.

'You liked it before you knew all that.' She turned a cold eye on him.

'True.'

'And all organic, no GM ingredients.'

'I am truly impressed.'

Her eyes narrowed.

'Honest,' he surrendered with a laugh. 'It's amazing.'

She nodded, satisfied. 'I make a mean salsa.'

He hadn't been talking about the sauce. But he leaned

back and watched her work, listened, more interested than he'd thought he'd be as she went on about the nutritional value of the ingredients. 'How do you know all this?' he finally interrupted the never-ending flow of facts as she poured ladlefuls into the masses of sterilised jars that waited on the table.

'I did lots of research about cancer-fighting superfoods and stuff. Tomatoes are up there.'

'Was your grandfather sick for a while?' Gabe held his breath as he waited for her answer. It was the first directly personal question he'd asked since that night when she'd sleepily muttered too few secrets.

She nodded briefly, her mouth closing, and she got very busy filling the jars. Totally shutting that topic of conversation down again. He tried not to frown, went for the obvious distraction instead.

'What do you want?' That flash of blue again from under the fluttering lashes.

'Payment for letting you use the kitchen,' he said in his worst lecherous-landlord tone.

'What kind of payment?' She smiled but he also saw the spark.

It was so easy to excite her. But so damn hard to open her up in other ways.

'Three bottles of that sauce.' He watched, his body helplessly winching harder when he saw the hint of disappointment in her eyes. He just couldn't resist. 'And...'

'And?' Her mouth tilted.

Gabe slapped a booklet on the table in front of her after dinner. 'Ever seen this?'

Roxie read the title. And frowned.

'It's the road code,' he drawled. 'And you need to study it, because you're going for your theory test tomorrow.'

'Am not.'

'Are too. Or else.'

She narrowed in on his naughty vibe. 'Else what?'

'We won't be checking any more items off your list.'

She gasped at his 'I mean it' expression. 'You're bluffing.'

He sat back, patted his lap for her as if she should come sit astride it. 'Come try and tempt me.'

The heat began to rise upwards, her chest, her neck, her face. But she wasn't going to let him tease her into saying yes to his bossiness. 'Don't need to. I can figure some fun for myself.'

'Think you'll find going solo isn't nearly so sweet now, Roxie,' he taunted.

She swiped up the damn book and opened it on a random page. Just so she could bury her burning face in it. Because she knew he was so right.

'You can do the practical in my car if you like.' He resumed the conversation as if he knew full well she wasn't concentrating on the printed words. 'Might be easier? I can get you covered on the insurance.'

Ugh, insurance. She hated that word. 'Thanks, but no, I couldn't.'

'You're too scared to drive something that actually goes fast?'

'I think you know I'm not afraid of fast.' She shot him a look over the boring rule book.

'Everything comes back to sex with you, doesn't it?'

'Are you *complaining*?' she mocked, tossing the road code aside. 'We *are* sex, Gabe. We're a shag team.' But she wasn't being completely honest—not even to herself. She got up from the table quickly. 'I've got the most awesome dance flick ever for tonight.'

'Oh, I can't wait.' Gabe didn't sound any less sarcastic than he had a moment before.

But the opening theme had barely started when his phone beeped. He glanced at the message and groaned.

'What's wrong?' She pressed pause on the remote, the opening number wasn't one to be missed.

He was studying the screen intently, scrolling through some lengthy missive. 'One of the boys has gotten into trouble. Cheating while on summer tour. Pretty sordid too, going to be all over the front pages tomorrow.' He shook his head and tossed his phone to the floor. 'This is why they shouldn't get married. Commitment doesn't work with this lifestyle.'

Roxie giggled. 'Are you serious?'

'Absolutely.' He met her smile with censure in his dark eyes. 'The pressure these guys are under? They're away so often. There's all that adrenalin—they need a release. Distance relationships never work and in this business there are even more factors to make marriages fail.'

Roxie gaped at his earnest expression. 'You call this lifestyle working with a *distance* relationship?' she mocked. 'Gabe, you're not talking being away months or even weeks at a time. You're talking *days*.'

'You don't understand the temptation they face.'

'Oh, please. Temptation passes *you* on the street every day. The number of women who give you that *look*.' She shook her head. She'd seen it so many times at the stadium. 'The guys who give into temptation on a short trip like that would give into it at home just as quick if the opportunity arose,' she said bluntly. 'It's not the lifestyle that's the problem, it's that the guy doesn't know how to keep his zipper up.' She chuckled again. 'I mean, really, Gabe, you're away for what, a week at most?'

'When we go on tours it's weeks at a time,' he said defensively.

'Oh, come on, it's a big fat excuse and you know it.' She leaned closer, getting into the stride of her argument now. '*You* don't want to give up your freedom in case something better swings along. That's okay, you don't have to. Just don't try to hide behind your job as some lame excuse for being unable to make a commitment. If you wanted to, you would. But you don't want to.'

That was right. He didn't. Gabe was stunned with how she had him pegged. And that she'd just shot him down with a couple of snappy sentences. Yes, he liked the convenience of the short-term fling—and the out-of-town bender was even better. No mess in his backyard. 'Okay, you're right. It took a lot to get my freedom and, no, I won't give that up for anyone. I'm not willing to compromise on the most important things in my life.' That was still his view, right?

She nodded, apparently all understanding now. 'I know exactly how you feel. I don't regret any of the time in the last few years. I'd still be doing it if I could. But now? I want my time. I want *my* freedom. I don't want anybody holding me back.' She grinned impishly.

Strangely, even though she was now agreeing with him, Gabe didn't feel any better. 'So you're really serious about the no-marriage-and-kids thing?'

'I think I take after my mother,' she said, settling more comfortably on the sofa. 'She didn't want me despite going ahead to have me. I'm not doing that to anyone. I'm never having any in the first place.'

'No permanent man either?' He had no idea why his pulse had just picked up.

She shook her head. 'Playmate every now and then. That's the way forward.'

She was quoting his own philosophy but it sounded so wrong coming from her mouth. He didn't like her turning her back on the idea of being with someone for good. She should be cherished and treasured and adored—the prize, the heart, of some guy's life. And any guy who even thought of straying from Roxie would need his head read. Who'd ever want to give her up?

Gabe really needed to bury this line of thought—it was weird. He pressed the pause button on the remote she still held so the movie started running again. But a dance flick was hardly the kind of movie to completely absorb him, so those damn thoughts kept circling. Had he been hanging back from doing anything more with any of his exes in case someone better came along? Surely not, he'd just thought he had it sussed. Even after the Diana debacle he'd merely figured all he had to do was fling it with the right kind of woman. But Roxie wasn't that kind. In fact he now wondered whether that kind of woman even existed.

Yet here Roxie was basically trying to walk in his foolish footsteps. That just didn't sit right with him.

Damn it, none of this was right.

CHAPTER TEN

As Roxie drove towards home she saw Gabe jogging through the park. He signalled and she pulled over. He raised a brow at the P-plate on the rear window. She'd known he'd spot it straight away.

'I didn't just do the theory, I passed my practical. First time,' she said smugly.

'I should hope so,' he answered drily as he got in the passenger seat. 'You've been driving on the roads long enough.'

Roxie giggled and drove the final few metres to the garage. It had been a brilliant day: she'd taken the afternoon off work and done her test, gone to practice with the Blades, they'd asked her to do some freestyle—to help work out a new routine. Now she'd come home and found *him*. And he'd just gotten out and opened the heavy old garage door for her to park the car and was waiting to close it once she was in. First time ever anyone had done it for her. Life just couldn't get better. Her smile widening, she stepped out to meet him. And her foot sank into a puddle. Several inches deep and lapping—water was flowing in from somewhere. She headed straight for the boxes sitting in the new lake.

'Maybe we left a hose on.' Gabe disappeared out of the side door. He was back in a nanosecond but the sound of running water hadn't ceased. 'Probably a burst pipe, won't take anything to fix,' he said, pulling his phone from his shorts pocket.

Only money she didn't have. She should have been saving everything—not having her hair done or buying multiple bottles of Bollinger. She should have waited until she had more resources to deal with these seemingly inevitable setbacks. The house had eaten all her resources over the last year; she'd really hoped she'd hit the end of it. This was supposed to be her new start. Angered with her idiocy, she splashed forwards to lift the first of the boxes to safety out in the garden. The contents of the ones at ground level must be sodden already.

Gabe had his phone to his ear; she could hear the 'on hold' music as she walked. 'You should move into the Treehouse while this dries out,' he said.

She shook her head. No way would she move in with Gabe. Her instinct had been whispering a warning to pull back on the time she spent with him and at that suggestion it shrieked. 'It's just a flood. Upstairs isn't damaged, only the stuff stored down here. It won't take long to dry.' She hoped. She also hoped like hell the plumber wasn't going to cost a bomb.

'You might want to transfer some of this stuff to plastic boxes for longer-term storage, especially the paperwork,' he said.

Did he think she hadn't considered that first time round? Of course she should have used better storage when she'd originally sorted all the stuff, but the banana boxes had been free from the supermarket. She didn't bother answering—the man was made of money, he had no clue what it was like for those not born with silver spoons.

'Don't do that.' He frowned at her. 'I'll lift them for you—' He broke off as someone finally took him off hold.

Roxie kept lifting and lugging—they were her boxes after all. Gabe's frown deepened as she marched back and forth past him carrying the worst affected out to the deck. She listened to him issue instructions to the plumber with his innate lord-of-all authority. Which annoyed her even more. She couldn't ask him not to make the call, didn't want to reveal her proximity to the poverty line, but she couldn't let the entire property flood either. As he wrapped the call she bent down for the next box—the bottom one of the first tower. The water was already at the one-third mark. She hoisted it up, cold wet running down her arm.

'Oh, hell,' she muttered, quickly changing her grip, but it was too late—the box simply disintegrated and its contents splashed everywhere. Glancing down at it all, her blood froze. She immediately looked for his reaction. Tension twisted his usual good-humoured expression. She could see him thinking, his face hardening as his jaw clamped, his eyes darkening.

Did he doubt her?

Defensiveness rose, intensified by tortured memories and the frustration from this latest fix-it job the house demanded. Truthfully she'd forgotten that box was even there. She'd had to. But his icy attention was fixed on the stuff now scattered, half submerged, over the floor and that defensiveness burst from her in a bitter torrent. 'I'm not a junkie, Gabe.'

He went all the more rigid. 'I know that,' he said roughly.

Given the number of plastic-wrapped syringes, blister packs of prescription-only painkillers, bottles of morphine and who knew what else, she wouldn't really have blamed him for wondering.

'They were your grandfather's,' he said shortly.

She bent, scrambling to get it all together. 'I meant to take it to a pharmacy to get rid of, but I just boxed and forgot it.'

'I can drop it off.' He bent down beside her and gathered the needles.

'He was diabetic,' she felt compelled to explain. 'Injections a couple times a day. Then pain relief too. Some of the pills were Grandma's.' It really did look as if she were running some kind of drugs lab. 'She had so many they took an age to dispense.'

'Why did it have to be you?' he asked. 'Where were the district nurses?'

'Busy.' Her defensiveness resurged—higher. '*I* could manage. Grandad didn't want to die in hospital so at the end I didn't call anyone. I gave him the painkiller the doctor prescribed and I held his hand and I watched him. In the end I called an ambulance because…' Because she couldn't bear it any more. She paused and tried to suck back her emotion. 'By the time it got there, he'd gone. That's a decision I made and I live with.'

She'd fought so damn hard with her stupid garden with her organic everything, and trying to make him laugh and do everything and anything anyone said might help battle that bastard disease. And for a couple of years there she'd succeeded. She'd thought it would go on like that indefinitely—what a dream that had been. Because all of a sudden he'd deteriorated and there had been no coming back from it. She looked up from the dirty puddle. 'It happens all the time. Cancer is the country's number one killer. People cope.'

'Most people don't have to cope alone,' Gabe answered gruffly, his hands full.

She shrugged, fully regretting revealing the little she just had to him. 'There was so much bad stuff happening in the city at that time, the medics were run off their feet.'

Gabe nodded but said nothing more. His pallor surprised her—for a doctor he looked a little shaken by all the medical guff. Tight-lipped, he stood and got a plastic bag to tip it all into. Then came back and viciously chucked the remainder in too.

Roxie blinked at the energy crackling off him. He was angry? Well, so was she. She didn't want to deal with this—least of all in front of him. She was so sick of fighting to keep this place okay. She picked up the box that had her mother's letters and papers in. She'd put it down here after it had given her nothing but disappointment. Not a single clue as to who her father had been. That dream had died a year ago too. 'I'll take some of these boxes upstairs,' she said dismissively.

'You don't want me to help you carry them up?' he called after her.

'No, I'm fine.'

Really? Gabe wasn't so sure about that—he heard raw emotion in her bitten-off words. 'It wouldn't take me a minute.'

'You've already done enough calling the plumber.'

Yeah, and she didn't exactly sound grateful about that. Gabe gritted his teeth, feeling extremely pissed off and it was worsening with each second. 'It really wouldn't take a minute.'

'I can manage.' She had her back to him, box in arms, stomping up the stairs already.

'I can help,' he argued. He hated her stubborn insistence on managing all by her damned self. She'd had to manage all kinds of hell as the primary carer, for not one, but two terminally ill elderly people. Alone. Why couldn't she say yes to a bit of muscle to help lug some bloody boxes now? Why couldn't she smile and say 'sure' and 'thanks'?

She looked over her shoulder, shooting him a quelling look. 'I don't need you to.'

Don't want you to, was what she really meant.

Gabe flung the bag of drugs into the corner of the garage. He could hear her stropping around up in her postage-stamp-sized studio. His fists clenched. There'd been no need for her to get snippy with *him*—the pipes weren't his fault, despite his random wish that she'd move in with him, he hadn't tampered with the plumbing like some sick stalker. But from years of working with finely balanced athletes, Gabe knew that a bad mood was often aggravated by not enough food. She must have gone straight from work to her driving test and then to the Blades practice. She had to be hungry. So he'd feed her. He wanted her to accept *something* from him tonight—and not merely sex.

He knocked on her door an hour or so later. For once she answered almost right away but that wasn't what made him blink so rapidly. No, she'd changed into the most hideous trackpants he'd ever seen, and, given he worked with sportsmen, he'd seen some ratty trackies. These were thick, massive and shapeless and he really just wanted to remove them then and there. But he reminded himself that wasn't the first priority.

'I'm guessing you probably haven't made dinner so I made enough for you too.' He refused to be offended if she said no to him. Even if he had gone to a stupid amount of effort.

'You have?' She blinked at him.

He nodded. 'It's on the deck if you want to come and get it.'

She hesitated.

'It's getting cold and I've gone to a lot of trouble.' He put on some pressure with a wicked look. He wanted to see her smile.

And she did smile—all sceptical, as if she didn't believe he'd ever go to any trouble. Oh, the irony.

'Okay, give me a second.' Roxie stepped back inside and shut the door. Gabe had gotten over his snappy temper flare, surely she could too. Hopefully he'd forgotten her angst moment in the garage. She was too tough to let a blasted pipe get her down—so it would delay her trip another couple of weeks perhaps; worse things had happened. She grabbed the half-bottle with the D on it—that and Gabe back in stud mode would help bubble her out of the funk.

'Wow,' she said, taking in the laden plates on the outdoor dining table. 'Not sure the Bolly is good enough for this.'

'Don't get too effusive.' He pulled out her chair. 'It's only burger and chips.'

'Not your average burger and chips.' She sat, breathing in the yum display. They were home-made bean patties, ripped-from-the-plant salad and freshly dug new potatoes cooked then crisped up something yummy. Her mouth watered, her appetite suddenly screaming. 'You cooked all this?'

'I'm a single man, living alone,' he drawled. 'You didn't think I could cook?'

'But it's—'

'Veggie, I know. Not bad for a beef-farm boy, huh?' He popped the cork and poured the champagne into two glasses—frowning when that was enough to empty the bottle.

She picked up her fork and took a bite of the patty poking out from the toasted roll. Oh, wow. 'You really made this from scratch?'

'Your amazement is insulting.'

She chuckled, warmth trickling back into her chilled body. 'I've never met anyone who makes veggie burgers like these. From scratch. Not even me.'

He pulled his phone from his pocket and swiped the screen a few times. 'Okay, I got the recipe online. Here.'

She angled her head to read the page he'd pulled up. 'The *Heganator*?' She didn't just giggle, she squealed. '*He*gan?'

'Yeah, cool recipes for the hot vegan male.' He turned the phone back to study it, oh, so intently. Then he peered over the top of the phone, eyes twinkling. 'I think it's really written by a woman. Apparently hegans like burgers and barbecues.'

'You're hot but you're not a hegan,' she said, almost all her old flirt tone back.

'But I can cook like one on occasion.'

'It is amazing. I mean that in a good way.' She looked at him and her teasing smile died. 'Thank you.'

Her heart was beating too hard. She couldn't remember when someone else had cooked dinner for her. When someone had gone to so much trouble and thought. Someone who bothered to understand what she preferred to eat and not eat. Certainly not her lame ex-boyfriend. The joke died from his eyes too—leaving them warm and gentle and so deep...

She dropped her knife so she had the excuse to break away from that acute, wordless communication. Surely she was reading the wrong messages. It wasn't caring she was supposed to see in him, it was supposed to be all carnal. But for a weird second there everything had gone upside down and inside out.

'While I have this out, I want your number,' he said.

She looked back up at him.

'Mobile number,' he elaborated at her blank expression. 'I'm away for the next week, so I need your number. In case.'

In case of what? 'I don't have one.'

'You don't have a mobile?' He leaned forward.

'Don't have any kind of phone.' She chased a bit of patty round the plate with her fork. 'Don't need one.'

'Of course you need one,' he said, still sounding amazed. 'Everyone needs one.'

'Well, I don't.' It was an expense she didn't need. The very few calls she had to make were usually local, so she made them from the gift shop.

'Roxie, it's a safety issue as much as anything. What if your ancient car breaks down when you're on some back country road?'

'I don't drive back country.' She smiled.

'You know what I mean.' He didn't smile back. He growled. 'You should have a phone.'

She didn't have a phone because she didn't have anyone to call. And that was the way it was going to stay.

'If I hadn't been here tonight, how would you have gotten hold of a plumber?' he asked, still holding his phone mid-air as he waited for her to answer.

'I would have figured something out,' she answered frigidly. She always had before. Tonight if she'd been alone she'd have turned off the water at the mains and waited 'til she had the money to deal with it. She stabbed a potato and stuffed it in her mouth. Having to chew stopped her saying too much more about her ability to manage just fine and about her funding issues. She didn't want him to know all that. He put his phone down and mirrored her actions, attacking his burger as if it were alive and about to scuttle off the plate away from him.

Several minutes later, both meals almost entirely eaten, Gabe spoke. 'Want to go out tonight?' His humour-laced attitude was back; so was his sinful smile. 'I'm guessing you haven't had nights and nights out on the club scene. I know a couple of places.'

Roxie's blood burned, but the melt from ice to fire was so rapid it hurt. Maybe dinner with Gabe hadn't been such a great idea—she felt wobblier now than when she'd first seen the water washing over the garage floor. As if her world were more on the edge of danger in this seemingly easy instant. 'I went dancing with the Blades after that first game. You know, the night you decided to go home early.' She matched his light'n'teasy tone.

'Another time.' He shrugged, that smile widening. 'But I confess I saw these poking out from that last box on the garage.' He bent and picked up something under his side of the table.

'Oh, I remember those.' She studied the couple of old records he held up and felt the ice threaten her heart again. She'd played those to her grandfather in the last few days as he'd slipped in and out of consciousness.

'No doubt you have a player up in that overcrowded antique shop you call your studio.'

'Somewhere under a million other things.' She didn't want to dig it out.

'No matter.' He put the vinyl records back by his seat and picked up his phone again. 'Because I found a couple of tracks online and downloaded them.' He tapped the screen and the intro started. 'Come on, you can't deny me when I cooked you that *amazing* dinner.'

In the end Roxie pushed her chair out and took his hand because it was herself she couldn't deny—she ached for the pleasure of his touch. She wanted a return to that simple, mindless, *uncomplicated* pleasure. Her bare feet were mud-splattered, her ugliest trackies hung shapelessly from her hips and her hair was a tangled mess. But he held her as if she were Cinderella herself in all her finery—only extra firm, as if he wasn't about to let her run away.

He danced smooth and natural and strong. Clearly not intimidated by her ballet background, he was in charge and not afraid to let her know it. She liked it more than she'd thought she would. She'd danced alone for years, but being partnered, guided like this? It was surprisingly good. The song was a big-band swing number from the nineteen fifties, one she'd always loved, one that brought happy with the sad in her mind's eye. But there was no room for memory, there was only now. He swept her from one side of the deck to the other, turning her on a coin-sized spot and all with the ease of a professional. Breathless, she pulled back to look in his face.

He shook his head ruefully. 'You didn't think I could dance either? Don't think I'm capable of anything much other than sex, do you?'

There was an edge to his comment that pushed Roxie's caution button. She thought him capable of a hell of a lot actually—thought he was more magnificent than was good for either of them. She didn't need to be wowed further by his cooking and dancing talents. It wasn't fair of him, not when this was supposed to be a trifling fling.

'Are you fishing for compliments?' she murmured lightly. 'You, the doctor who has all those dancers faking injuries to get near you?'

She felt the slight movement in his chest, guessed it

to be a grunt of amusement. He pulled her closer to keep her moving. Another song automatically played from his phone. Another swing number, slower this time. She let her lashes droop as he swayed with her, felt the stresses from the flood ease. So easy to lean against him, so easy to let him take all her weight, to take all this and more from him… But he didn't want to give more. And if she did that, if she let herself *depend*, then she'd want more. And wasn't she determined *not* to want that from anyone? It would only end badly. Being too close always brought loss and that was what she wanted to be free of most of all.

'Do you want to talk about it?' he asked softly, his smooth voice inviting every confidence.

Roxie stared over his shoulder at the top of the trees. What *man* ever wanted to *talk*? Men hated that emotional 'talking' thing, didn't they? They were all action over words. Then she realised—this wasn't Gabe acting like a *man*, this was Gabe acting like a *doctor*. Was he taking care of her because he felt sorry for her, because he'd found out something more about her time with her grandfather's last days? Was he cooking for her and offering to counsel her too? Was he afraid she was fragile? That she might go deep depressive as Diana had? It was nice he was concerned and all, but *medical* concern wasn't what she wanted from him.

Ever.

So no, she didn't want to talk. She didn't want anything from him. She pulled free and stepped out of his arms. 'Actually I'm pretty tired,' she said coolly.

'Okay,' he said. There was a silence as she took another step back and didn't meet his eyes. He stood exactly where she'd left him, as if he was waiting—for what? There was nothing she could bear to give. And she couldn't take anything more tonight either.

'I have some dishes to do,' he said eventually, quietly.

That hit her conscience. 'Oh, I should—'

'No, my mess, my shame,' he answered with a brief facsimile of a smile. 'You're not seeing it.'

Now she looked at him—and with superhuman effort refrained from asking him to come up with her. For now, contrarily, she didn't want to be alone. Now she wanted back in his arms. For a second there she'd glimpsed something so sweet, but it was a mirage lasting only while the music played. If she took him now, she'd be vulnerable to investing too much as he'd warned her before their first time together. She couldn't chase a dream that would disappear in a blink and a smile. Her bruised heart would be battered worse than ever. Exactly what she didn't want. So she turned and took the stairs alone.

Frustrated, Gabe let her go, at a loss as to how else he could try to break through the defensive barriers that she could erect in the blink of an eye. Lying alone in bed, he watched the light at her window. It was after two in the morning before she switched it off. Less than four hours later he heard her flick the hose on in the garden. He was due at the airport soon and he'd be in Sydney for the next five nights and, damn it, he wanted to reach out to her.

He walked out of the house, saw her pallor and the dark rings beneath her eyes. She couldn't completely hide her stress. The pipes would be nothing to fix, he'd already paid the plumber to come back later today and finish last night's temporary patch, but as for the other hurts he suspected went deep? He didn't know how to help with those, not when she wouldn't admit to them—least of all to him. But he wanted to. He really wanted to.

She tossed the hose and strode to meet him. Her bruised eyes burned, feminine aggression made her slim frame strong—and made him unusually weak at the knees. She didn't give him the chance to say anything. No, she led the dance and reverse cowgirl rocked. It really did. He loved watching her half-lightened, half-natural coloured hair swinging over her back. Loved tracing the curve of her butt. Loved sliding his hands around to her breasts, down her slender ribs and beyond to her hottest spot, teasing the ecstasy out of her. But he wanted to look into her eyes too. Wanted to *know* her—to connect so much more completely than this.

He knew she was determined and today more aggressive than ever—more hungry, more driven, more demanding. Her hands were so tight on his thighs he'd bear her fingermarks for days. For someone so slight she had gut-wrenching strength and she ripped what she wanted from him. He growled through gritted teeth, desperately holding back as she rode him. Glad there were no neighbours overlooking them—given they were outside, given it was six in the morning, given this was all screaming, sweaty, animal sex. But the best sex of his life wasn't enough any more.

She arched as her orgasm hit, her piercing shriek loud enough to make the sparrows fly from the trees. As soon as she crumbled he moved, flipping her over and then rolling again so she was back above him, but facing him this time. He held her face so he could see into those sex-dazed eyes and pushed as deep as he could go.

He waited, breathing hard while he got it together. Because he refused to have sex with her now. Now he was making love. Now he was giving everything he could.

Her eyes widened, she shook her head, but he firmed his grip, holding her so she couldn't escape his kiss. And slowly, so slowly he started all over again. Every movement, every touch filled with care and passion. His hands sweeping, fingers drifting, his heart bursting. He ached for completion, contentment—hers. He wanted to fill her, to treasure her.

She lay limp above him—as if she was sated already and could move no more. So he was gentle, slow. And then he felt the subtle change, her skin warming as muscle beneath became energised. She draped like silk now—her limbs curving, embracing. Her hands cupped almost shyly. And then he heard her breathy sob—it wasn't an entirely sexual plea. He cradled her and kissed her, the simplest of caresses. Until that moment when she moaned, until she clung, until she murmured his name brokenly just that once. Until she was soft, warm, accepting. And his.

He groaned as words failed, emotion overwhelming him—the need for her, to care for her. But also, for her to care back. He wanted it *all* back from her. Oh, now he felt it—the yawning need that had never before been realised, let alone exposed. So vulnerable.

He pulled her closer, buried his face in her warm soft skin, and gave in to it.

Afterwards her eyes remained firmly closed. Apparently she was asleep. He sat up, managed to hook one arm under her legs, while supporting her back with the other. He carried her to the comfort of a soft mattress and cotton coverings and space. To *his* bed, not hers. She didn't open her eyes as he covered her and told her to sleep. But he knew she was awake. He could feel the aware tension emanating from her body. But there was no time left to call her on it.

CHAPTER ELEVEN

GABE sat in his hotel room in Sydney and ruefully laughed about the plans he'd made only a couple of weeks ago about coming here and having some seriously debauched nights on the town. Had he honestly thought he could sate his sexual appetite with a one-night stand? The idea of sex with a stranger left him cold—and flaccid. He pulled out his phone and went online. Pointless given she didn't have any kind of a phone, let alone a computer. So he did a search to find clips from Blades' shows. Naturally some fan had uploaded the Blades' on-pitch performance from the first week. He watched it. Watched it again. After three replays knew exactly when each shot of Roxie was with her long, slender legs lifting and her hair wild and her cheeks flushed and her smile huge. Roxie dancing only moments after he'd been pawing her in the corridor. The sexiest woman ever.

Not so flaccid now.

He might have dated a couple of dancers before, but he'd never been reduced to watching vids of any woman over and over. He pushed the button so the screen went black. Lay back on his bed, the phone pressed to his chest. He hated that she'd not said a word this morning. That she'd used him. He had more to offer her than that and he wanted her to realise it, want it, accept it.

Only now distance brought doubts. Had he imagined the warmth and caring in her return embrace? He needed to know her emotions were as entangled as his.

He sat up, frustrated with his impotence. Surely there was something he could do? He glanced at the phone in his hand and smiled at the obvious. He scooped up his wallet and hotel keycard, thankful that the shops in this city were open all hours.

Roxie worked late at the shop, avoiding the emptiness back at the Treehouse. She knew the science of it. The way humans were programmed to respond to a prospective mate. Women the world over—regardless of their culture or background—displayed the same available signals to the potential male—innate, instinctive, unstoppable. So why wasn't she having any of those normal responses to any of those other guys? There were a ton of them in that stadium, several were gorgeous, certainly virile and fit. Couldn't get fitter. And yet there was none of that softening deep inside; she didn't catch herself giving any a second look. Hadn't been *compelled* to. Not that she'd been compelled to with Gabe. He'd been the right guy in the right place at the right time, that was all. There was nothing any more special about him than anyone else. Right?

But then there'd been this morning. And there'd been nothing scientific about this morning. It had been all terrifying, out-of-control magic.

So she was relieved he'd gone away. She had time to remember her goals for her future—to travel and be independent. A free spirit with an unencumbered heart.

Finally she walked home, bypassing the heavy machinery that had trucked into the street some time during the day—diggers making mud and noise as they replaced broken waste water pipes. She understood the need, since the earthquakes that had decimated so much of the city, the repair and renewal work had been intense. She'd got off relatively lightly—her home mostly okay, her workplace mostly okay, so she wasn't going to complain about the roadworks now.

She went through the garage, planning to go straight upstairs, except she was drawn to the Treehouse. It looked sad somehow, as if it knew it was empty. Even the windows seemed sad. Then she realised that was because the one at the front was on a lean—sagging towards the tree. She put her head on an angle; it didn't help. She reached for her keys and opened up. Walked into the main room, to that window nearest the tree. Three quarters of the way there, the floor creaked alarmingly. She could see the tipping angle of the floor with her bare eyes. Under her weight it actually sagged an inch more.

She jumped back to a more secure part of the room. Oh, that could not be good. She raced outside again. She didn't need a spirit level to be certain that corner of the house had sunk. She couldn't believe it—not when it had survived all those earthquakes. Why was it crumbling now?

She looked up at the three-quarter-century-old branches and then down at the roots. She didn't know how bad it was yet, but she already knew she didn't have the money to fix it. She went back to the gift shop and called an engineering firm. They sent an engineer first thing next morning. She stood beside him, trying to keep a grip as he did his assessment. The foundations had gone. The tree roots had rotted, causing a giant hole beneath the house. It was possible the vibrations caused by the heavy machinery out on the road had exacerbated the rapid sink, but it would have happened soon anyway. And if it wasn't fixed, the whole house could come crashing down.

Roxie looked up at the branches—the thing that gave the house its beauty, its point of uniqueness, was the thing that would ultimately cause its destruction.

The engineer apologised as he explained—especially when she asked how much repairs could cost. He promised to send another engineer for a second opinion, but for now he was classing it as unsafe—*uninhabitable*—until the remedial work was done. Roxie's blood froze as she processed the info. Uninhabitable meant she'd lose Gabe as her tenant. Which meant she'd lose her income. The engineer left a brief report for her then and there. Black inked words leapt off the blinding white page—extensive, damage, cost...

Anger surged. She'd fought so long and still been defeated—in everything. She turned to the garden she'd tended for so long in the hope it could help her grandfather. But it had ultimately failed her too. The tall, fruitful plants mocked her, growing so strong when there was nothing left in her life. Furious, she lashed out with her bare hands. She tore the nearest tomato plant, swearing when the leaves ripped through her palms. She clawed until the whole thing was out, leaving a square of bare brown earth. She stopped, breathlessly stared at the small empty space that had been exposed.

Yeah, that was better.

Gabe frowned as the taxi drove alongside the park; there was something different about Roxie's place. When the car pulled over he saw the problem clearly. The hedge had been cut so there was a wide *path* through. He sprinted along it. 'Roxie? What's going on?'

He stopped, shocked, as he got to the garden.

'You're here sooner than I expected.' She clattered down the stairs from her studio in crazily high heels and met him with a smile, her hair flicking round her face. Only her eyes weren't sparkling to match.

'What the hell's happened?' Gabe all but gasped.

She carefully brushed her hair back behind her ears. He saw a long thin, scratch on the back of her hand. 'The vegetable garden was too big. No potential buyer would want it like that.'

Gabe still couldn't breathe. 'Potential buyer?'

She nodded blithely and stepped closer in her pretty dress. 'I'm selling.'

What? His heart stopped altogether.

'It's the right thing to do.' She smiled. 'I should have worked that out sooner.'

He stared back at the neatly turned over, empty soil— every abundant bed now completely cleared. She'd ripped out that entire magnificent garden. It was all gone. 'Oh, Roxie, what have you done?'

'Tidied up.' She laughed as if his reaction was over the top. 'It'll be bought by a developer anyway and the place will be skittled.'

What? Now his heart raced, thudding so hard in his ears he couldn't be sure what he was hearing—or what he was seeing.

'It's okay,' she reassured, sounding all confident. 'Take a look at the house.'

He stared at her instead. Because it wasn't okay. She could smile as much as she liked but she was never going to get him to believe this was okay.

She didn't fill the silence he left for her. Instead she waited and finally he turned and saw an official notice taped on the door. He'd seen a ton of them in the months post-earthquake. 'Why have they stickered it?'

'The foundations have gone,' she said matter-of-factly. 'It's sunk already. It could fall down any time.'

He could see the worst spot now, right by the tree. 'Foundations can be fixed.'

'Not this time.'

He couldn't believe this was happening. He couldn't believe she was acting so calm when he knew, he just knew she was being eaten up inside. He whirled to face her, to look into that too perfectly *made-up* face. 'You don't have to sell it.' She really didn't.

'I can't afford to fix it.'

He coughed away the tight feeling in his throat. 'What about insurance?'

She smiled again, that awful smile that was nothing but a meaningless twist to her mouth. 'There is no insurance, Gabe. We couldn't afford it. I was only working sporadically because—'

She broke off, but Gabe knew why already. Because her grandfather had been sick and she'd been needed at home with him here.

'There's no insurance for the car, the house or the contents and I don't have any savings.' She still wore that synthetic smile. 'We were lucky in the earthquake that there wasn't much damage. I've spent the last year fixing the superficial stuff. I tried to get insurance after but the companies weren't exactly running to cover any houses then and honestly I still couldn't afford it. I can't afford the repairs.'

'Roxie—'

'I'm sorry about your tenancy,' she interrupted him. 'Not much of a welcome after your trip away. You can't stay in there tonight.'

'If I can't stay there, you're not staying either,' he said. He'd take her somewhere with him and work on her until she broke down and let out the agony he was sure was hidden behind her dull eyes.

'No, I'm not. My flight goes at three p.m. tomorrow.'

'What?' Oh, no, no, no. This was worse than anything.

'I've brought my trip forward.'

It was more of a shock than seeing how she'd decimated her beloved garden. 'What about your job?'

'I've resigned already.' Still that smile.

'What about the Blades?'

'That's why they have an extra in the squad. They're used to losing dancers partway through the season.' Now the smile had the slightest of edges.

What about me? Gabe wasn't going to ask that. 'So you're going to run away?'

'I'm not running away.' Finally there was a spark in her eyes—a flash of temper. Good, he wanted more of that honest kind of emotion.

'I'm getting on with my life,' she said. 'There's nothing here for me any more.'

Okay, maybe he didn't want *that* honest. 'I'm nothing?'

There was a moment. One moment when something else flashed before that damn smile came back, that caricature of Foxy Roxie sass. 'Not nothing, Gabe, you've been an education.'

His head went all funny, his breathing fast and shallow, he couldn't *think* properly. She still saw him as nothing but a good-time guy? An *education*—with his sexual *effort* and all? 'I think there's a bit more to us, Roxie. Maybe you're too inexperienced to know that.'

She shook her head and added to that sassy smile with a vixen shimmy of her shoulders. 'I'm not too inexperienced to know that this isn't anything more than a fling. Neither of us ever wanted anything more.'

The Treehouse wasn't the only thing with shaky foundations. Gabe's world was sinking with every word she spoke.

'I could buy it,' he said, latching onto the house rather than facing the implications of his tumbling emotions.

'Please don't feel like you have to help me.'

'I don't. I want the house. I've always wanted the house.' And he wanted what belonged in it too.

She laughed. 'You don't want the house *now*. It's ruined.'

'It's not, it just needs new foundations.' He saw her stiffen and tried to fight it—he had to break down her damn defences somehow. 'I'm not doing this out of sympathy, Roxie.'

'You can't help yourself, Gabe,' she said patronizingly, maintaining that bloody smile. 'You're a *doctor*. Helping people is in your blood. It's so much a part of you, you don't even realise. But you help those players, you helped your sister. You pulled back from your social life because you were so bothered about hurting someone. You're a good guy, Gabe. But I'm not going to let you get all chivalrous over this just because you took my virginity. We're having sex because it's fun and it's all we want from each other. You don't need to do anything more for me, okay?'

How could she see that good in him—more than he deserved—and not want more from him?

'Don't try to dictate to me what I can and can't do,' he snapped. 'If I want to buy the house, I'll buy it.'

Even in the face of his temper she kept her cool, angling her head and looking up at him from beneath those darkened lashes. 'This is *my* problem, Gabe, not yours. You'll get your bond money back.'

'I don't care about the bloody bond money.'

She shook her head and laughed. 'Only you can afford not to care about money.'

'What's that supposed to mean?' His anger mounted—how could she maintain this veneer?

'You're so used to doing whatever you want, achieving what you want, getting whoever and whatever you want. Have you ever really had to fight for anything, Gabe?' Oh, now there was an edge, the slightest hint of cut in her tone.

'I've had my battles.'

'Breaking out from family expectation?' she teased.

Well, that wasn't as nothing as she made it sound when you were talking five generations of expectation, of being the sixth Andrew G. Hollingsworth and the only one to turn into Gabe. Of never feeling as if you could have your own voice. At the time, as a teen, it had been all but everything.

She laughed and answered her own question. 'All that did for you was get you even more used to having your own way.'

Yeah, he was totally used to getting what he wanted. But he was miles off getting it now. This was a first. This was not nice.

'Gabe, when you've fought some really tough battles, you know when something's worth that effort or not. And this place isn't worth my fighting for any more,' she said. 'It's right for me to leave it.'

He just didn't believe she meant that. 'Roxie—' He broke off when he saw her stiffen.

And that was when he knew. She might be bleeding to death inside, but her mind was made up and she was the strongest person he'd ever met. She'd chosen her path and she was running for it. So why try and stand in her way? If this was what she truly wanted, and apparently it was, why argue and make it harder for her? He'd only fail at it anyway.

She looked as if she hadn't slept at all the last couple of nights. Probably worrying and breaking her heart over losing the house. Now he was furious—she should have bloody gotten in touch with him. It hurt that she hadn't. Instead she'd made all these decisions already. On her own.

Was that because he wasn't important enough to her to talk to about it? He was merely a bedmate, nothing more than a toy for her? He had the horrible feeling it was. And there was one way of finding out for sure.

'I got you a little something when I was in Sydney,' he said, lightening his tone completely.

Her eyes widened in genuine surprise.

He dug the new phone from his pocket and handed it out to her. 'We can stay in touch. If you ever need anything…' He trailed off, momentarily floored by the frozen expression on her face. 'You don't need to worry about the ongoing costs or anything. I've got that covered.'

'Gabe, I can't accept this from you.'

Just the phone or anything he might offer? 'Sure you can.' He forced a smile. 'It has a great camera—you'll need that on your travels. I've downloaded some apps for you already, set up an account so you can get more, whatever you want.'

'Gabe…'

'You live in the mobile age, Roxie, you need one. It's a safety thing—see it can be a torch, an alarm, a GPS navigation system…' He was selling it too hard. Only because she looked more and more distanced. Not wanting to be rude to him, but clearly not wanting to even touch the thing. Oh, hell, he'd been right. The distress he read in her had nothing to do with him. She didn't want to know him once she'd gone.

'You can text me any time, send me a photo or something.' He pushed one last time for a reaction.

And at that she smiled and took the phone from him. 'You just want a sext pic, right?'

It was the worst attempt at humour he'd ever heard.

'Honestly, I just want you to be able to get in touch if you need to,' he said.

If she *wanted* to. Which clearly she didn't. He got it now. Oh, yeah, she was hurting, she was a mess inside. But not about *him*, it was all her house. He'd seen her a bit shaken up only last week over a simple burst pipe; he knew how much work she'd put into that garden, into keeping the place in shape, the furniture that had all that history. And she was gutted about losing it all.

But not about leaving him.

'I'd like to get in touch now,' she purred, stepping closer. 'There are still a few items on my list that we haven't ticked.' She actually pulled it out from her pocket and unfolded it.

Gabe didn't see the sheet for the red fog of fury that suddenly materialised before his eyes. 'You risked your neck going in there to get your sex list?' And she'd stashed it in her pocket so they could work through it together tonight? Irate, he glared at her make-up and her pretty dress and her fancy shoes—she'd got dolled up for her last debauched night with him? He really was just a tool to help tick off her list?

She looked slightly apologetic. 'Well, I would have

got your stuff but I didn't want to pry into your personal things.'

Oh, of course she didn't. The dinners, the movies on the sofa, the laughs, that last time they'd been together? All had meant nothing to her. It really was just a physical fling. A feel-good-for-the-moment thing. She was keeping her innermost emotions at a distance and using him as some kind of take-the-edge-off crutch?

'I think it'll be okay if you just zip in and out to get your personal items quickly,' she added, spreading her hands wider over his torso. 'But you should probably get the construction guys in hard hats to retrieve the furniture and stuff.'

As if she were really that concerned for his welfare? She just wanted his damn body.

'Come up to the studio with me,' she murmured. Her lashes dropped as she watched her fingers sliding across his chest. 'I've got that last bottle of Bolly we can share.'

He couldn't believe she really wanted that now. She wanted to use him so she could forget the hurt of losing her house?

Hell, no. She wasn't getting everything her own way. Not any more.

He tipped up her chin and looked into those mascara-framed, listless eyes. Bent and kissed her. Her arms slipped around him instantly, her lithe body melting, twisting, teasing against his already. It'd be so easy to fall deeper into her delicious heat, to take what was being offered. But what was on offer wasn't enough. He wasn't doing it to himself. If it was over, then it was over *now*. He had some pride. He wasn't going to be a boy-toy for her right up to the minute she was ready to discard him and step onto some plane. He had some self-respect.

And he was angry.

'Those bottles aren't really big enough for sharing,' he said, trying to keep a lid on it. Trying to ignore how badly his body wanted him just to give in. 'And I don't think there's anything more I can teach you now.'

Roxie watched him stalk over to the house. Her pride reared up, she knew what Gabe liked and wanted. It was what she wanted too. To be free to have some fun. And she'd wanted to get through this last horrendous night having fun with the one guy she knew in the world capable of doing just that. Hell, she thought it was the *only* way she might get through tonight—in a state of mindlessness. And she desperately, desperately wanted to feel him that one last time. Because she wasn't doing this ever again.

Only he'd just said no. And she was devastated.

She ran up the stairs to the garage to hide before the hit registered and she lost some of her tightly held composure. She faced the almost empty room. She'd sold all the furniture to an antique store—cheaply as she was in such a hurry. And she'd sold the car. That was how she'd gotten her airfare.

She looked down from the emptiness to the phone in her hand. The same as his, fancy and beautiful only he'd gotten hers a sleek silver case. Girly and gorgeous. Unable to resist, she pressed the button to turn it on. He'd loaded a picture of the Blades as her wallpaper. She tested the ringtone. It was the song they'd danced to just the other night. She opened up the contacts. There was only one programmed already. Gabe Hollingsworth. There was a picture and everything. One he'd obviously snapped himself—with a more self-conscious grin than she'd ever seen on him in the flesh. More handsome than ever. She couldn't bear it.

Glancing up, the first thing she landed on was the

fridge. It mocked her with its remaining half bottle of Bolly. She opened the fridge door and chucked the phone in the ice-box in the top. Slammed the door and backed away from it as if it were some bomb she had to freeze to disarm.

Which was how she had to deal with him all over.

Gabe had hit a new low of voyeurism. Standing at the window in his darkened room in the damaged house, he watched her put the phone in the fridge and slam the door. His jaw dropped. Not exactly what he'd expected. But why was he surprised? She was putting all her feelings on ice. And didn't she do everything to the extreme? She wasn't just vegetarian, she was vegan. She didn't just have a vegetable plot, she had a vegetable paddock. When she'd decided to get a gig dancing, she went for the biggest, flashiest show in town. When she'd decided she wanted him as her lover, she'd been fearless in her pursuit. But when things were finished, they were totally finished. No looking back—like her decision to sell the house, the car, everything. No phone, no contact. All or nothing.

And she'd put him in the nothing box.

Too many long hours later, he waited at the bottom of her stairs. She appeared mid-morning. Looking awful but beautiful, hiding the lack of sleep damage beneath a layer of make-up thick enough to withstand a nuclear detonation.

'I'm giving you a ride to the airport.' He stood to let her past, his body stiff from sitting so long.

'That'd be great.' She cracked a smile through the warpaint.

So that was how they were playing it, as if it were all still fun and friendly and meaningless. He'd take her to the airport and let her go, right? It wasn't fair to try to hold someone back—he knew just how much resentment could build when someone tried to clip your wings.

'Got your phone?' he asked as casually as he could given he had shards of glass in his throat.

The smile stayed fixed as she nodded. He saw her gripping her hands together tightly, her fingers locked into each other. He made a thing of starting the engine and then clapped a hand on his forehead. 'Oh, I forgot something, hang on a mo.'

It took less than a minute to jog through the garage and up the stairs. He used the keys she'd just given him to hand to the lawyer. Apparently he could be trusted with that minion task. Her studio was all but empty—that furniture had already gone, and he'd noticed the car was gone from the garage too. It cut to the quick that she'd chucked the stuff that only days ago she'd held so tightly to her. Sure enough, the phone was there in the ice-box where she'd left it. She had no intention of keeping in touch with him. Gabe forced his blood to freeze, stopping the surging anger from flooding the deep wound she'd gouged inside him. He had to stay cool on this. So she was the first woman to dump him—maybe that was why he was so bothered. Maybe it was all just hurt pride.

Out of the corner of his eye he watched her stare straight ahead as he drove her away from the house she'd loved.

She didn't even blink.

Roxie didn't say a word the entire drive to the airport. Her throat had seized. It was too much to hope he'd just drop her in the two-minute car parks right outside the terminal. Of course he didn't. He parked in the expensive parks, insisted on carrying her bag in and even filled in a luggage tag for her while she checked in.

She was going straight through the security clearance; she couldn't delay getting away from him. She was about to lose it entirely. She folded her arms tight around herself, gripping her upper arms with her hands, holding all the agony inside.

It hurt to see him so at ease about her leaving. Which was yet more proof it was the right call to have made. She couldn't believe it when his expression warmed to tease-level as he cupped her face and tilted it up towards him.

Yeah, thank goodness he'd said no to her last night. From this one touch now, she knew she'd never have been able to pull off a last night of nothing but passion. She'd have clung to him, begging for everything he never wanted to give.

He'd meant the phone as a friendly gesture. It was kind of him. But she didn't want kind or friendly. He was supposed to be her *lover*. It was supposed to have been *once*. Only it had been once every which way and then some. And there'd been the fun, the conversation, the laughter, the way he'd held her, that had all led to… something she couldn't bear to define.

But he was redefining them in a way that was even worse. Concerned and caring, wanting to stay in touch as a *friend*. It was humiliating when what she really wanted was…

No.

She knew—to her *bones*—that she couldn't stay in touch with him. She was leaving this part of her life behind. If she really was going to live light and free, then she had to sever all connection.

'Your lawyer will be in touch about the sales of all

the assets,' he said quietly. 'But you know I'll keep an eye on it for you too.'

She nodded, mustered a slight smile to show her damn gratitude. Her throat was so tight with unshed tears she couldn't speak.

She looked for one last time into his beautiful almost black eyes. His teasing look gave way to a small smile that sawed through her nerves. She was a total block of wood, couldn't kiss him back, could barely manage to take the sweetness of his light, gentle caress. Gripped her sleeves even harder to stop herself shattering into a thousand little pieces of nothing.

'I hope it's everything you want it to be,' he whispered.

She barely nodded because now she knew—uselessly—that what she truly wanted was right in front of her. She wanted *him*—to love her, to want her, to hold her and keep her... But he didn't want to keep or be kept. And she couldn't bear the inevitable hurt of his rejection and her loss.

Motionless, she stared up at him. Stared so hard she could no longer focus. Her last sight of him blurred—he was that fuzzy outline she'd first seen in the bathroom that day. She blinked but it didn't make it better. She couldn't say a thing, her throat burning hot but, like the rest of her, paralysed.

She heard his deeply drawn breath. Felt his hands hard on her shoulders. 'Go.' Forcefully he turned her away. Pushed so she took a stumbling step in the direction of security clearance. Her frozen cold feet automatically took the next step. And the next.

She didn't turn, didn't raise a hand as she heard him harshly instruct her that one last time.

'Go.'

CHAPTER TWELVE

THE flight lasted a lifetime. The droning engine hurt her head. The air-conditioning left her eyeballs even drier. The chilled blood in her veins made her stiff and cold. After a hell-on-wheels stopover and yet another long, frozen flight they began the descent, except the lights of London stretched for ever. And hard as Roxie tried, she couldn't stop thinking about Gabe. Surely he'd seen it in her face? In that one moment her heart had been exposed, there for him to take. If he'd asked, she'd have stayed, she'd have literally fallen into his arms. Only he'd told her to go.

So go she did—to all the tourist attractions: Buckingham Palace, The Tower of London, Madame Tussauds... And at the end of her first, miserable week, mad with herself for still feeling wretched, she queued for tickets at Covent Garden to see the Royal Ballet, as she'd dreamed of doing for almost two decades.

The theatre itself was beautiful, the audience was beautiful, the ballerinas beautiful. But Roxie's heart wasn't in it. She watched the dancers—the incredibly talented dancers—and hated every second of it. In the interval she walked out through the well-lit foyer, out into the crowded, famous square. And that was when she drew up short, not knowing what the hell she was doing or should do or wanted to do. She was in the middle of a foreign city, utterly alone. Just as she'd thought she'd wanted to be.

Only to find it *sucked*.

She'd made the most massive mistake.

'Roxie.'

She turned. No one in this city knew who she was. No one in the world knew *where* she was. So who was calling out to her?

Okay, now she was seeing ghosts—because there was a guy standing just by the theatre entrance who looked exactly like Gabe. But he couldn't be a ghost because Gabe wasn't dead, he was back in New Zealand. So she must be hallucinating. Delayed jet lag was sending her crazy.

It was a pretty good hallucination, though, because now the Gabe-non-ghost was walking, his gaze trained on her. She blinked but he was still there, striding towards her, faster now, until he was almost upon her. And he was in the most gorgeous suit and clutching a glossy red programme.

'You don't like the ballet,' she said when he got within earshot, because what else *could* she say to this unreal creature?

'Yeah, but you do.' He stopped a mere ten centimetres away from her, his expression searching. 'Why have you walked out halfway through?'

'I didn't think it was realistic.' Although it seemed she'd lost her grip on what was real altogether because here she was talking to a hallucination and, incredibly, it was talking back.

His brows nearly hit his hairline. 'A girl gets let down by a guy so she dies of a broken heart. Then she comes back as a ghost and protects that guy from other supernatural spurned women. Which bit's not realistic?' The corner of his mouth rose in the smallest of grins.

Okay, so now she was sure she was dreaming. 'You *hate* ballet, so how come you know the story of *Giselle*?'

'Because I've sat through three performances already.' His smile widened to rueful and he stepped just that bit closer.

'Three?' Her voice almost failed as she felt the warmth of his breath on her icy skin.

'I'm sure the woman in the ticket office thinks I'm a stalker. Which I kind of am.'

Roxie stared at him, her mind spinning. He really wasn't a ghost. He really was here. Oh, Lord, *why* was he here?

'So which bit did you think was unrealistic?' he prompted her.

She was shaking inside, outside, all over. 'I didn't like how she died of a broken heart just because that guy let her down,' she whispered.

'No, that wasn't exactly brave of her,' he agreed softly. 'What should she have done instead?'

Roxie was still digesting his appearance, so she didn't answer. She just stared at him some more and tried not to think too closely about *why* he was here.

'What would you have done?' He waited for a while. Then offered an answer himself. 'Should she have packed her bags and gone adventuring instead?'

Roxie shook her head, spurred into a sturdier response at that. 'No, she should have confronted him and told him what for.' That was what she should have done. She should have told him what she really wanted—been honest and to be unafraid of the consequences.

'Fair enough.' Gabe's eyes were fathomless inky

pools. 'But you know, I think you'd find the second half better.'

'Why?' Her throat had seized so tight again she could barely answer, and the trembles were graduating to shudders.

'Because in that half she proves her strength,' he answered, still quiet. Still unfathomable. 'She does everything in her power to protect that guy because she loves him so much. And to be able to love someone that deeply, that passionately, is beautiful. It's rare and it's a gift.'

Her heartbeats boomed like cannons. She refused to believe this might be what she wanted it to be. She wanted it too much—she was still too scared to be honest and to be unafraid of the consequences. So she tried to joke, just in case. 'Are you saying you *enjoyed* the ballet?'

'Well,' he answered seriously, 'I saw some parallels.'

'I'm not about to die of a broken heart,' she said, suddenly indignant. She hated him thinking she was weak.

'I am so aware of that.' His grin flashed, even his melt-inducing laugh sounded briefly. 'That wasn't what I meant.'

Roxie couldn't take much more without losing it. 'Well, what *did* you mean?'

'That you're like her in that you have the capacity to love that deeply, that profoundly.'

Oh, now she felt hurt—and so, so vulnerable. 'What makes you think that?'

His expression softened. 'You showed it in the way you cared for your grandparents. You did everything and anything you could for them.'

'Nothing anyone else wouldn't have done.' She tried to minimise it; she was no saint.

He shook his head. 'You *give*, Roxie. You give everything.'

She didn't say anything to that. Couldn't.

He leaned nearer, bending slightly so their faces were almost touching, whispered, 'Aren't you going to ask me why I'm here?'

'Should I have to ask?' she basically wailed, her nerves finally shredded. 'You don't just want to tell me?'

'I shouldn't have let you down.' He too suddenly sounded rougher round the edges.

'You've *never* let me down.' Every cell inside her hurt from the effort of trying to stop trembling. To stay standing. He'd been wonderful to her in all the ways he could.

He closed his eyes. 'Yes, I have.'

Did he mean that final night when he'd refused her stupidly desperate advances? 'You were allowed to say no to me.'

'No.' His eyes flashed open, his gaze pinning her. 'I let you down, and myself down, when I let you leave without telling you how I felt. I should have told you, but I was proud. And hurt. Now I'm just so miserable I'm prepared to grovel as much as I have to.'

Roxie's shaking became uncontrollable. 'G-g-grovel?'

'You asked if I'd really had to fight for something. That if I had, I'd know when a fight was worth the effort. Well, I'm fighting now. You know what for?'

She shook her head. The boulder that had just gotten lodged in her throat prevented her answering verbally.

'I'm fighting for you.'

Gabe watched the colour wash out of her face—leaving her paler than when she'd first seen him walking towards her. 'I didn't want you to go,' he said roughly. 'I should have told you that, but I didn't want to *stop* you from going. I didn't want to stand in your way and I didn't think you wanted—' He broke off. She was still staring at him as if he were an apparition or something. He'd been holding back, not wanting to overwhelm her but it wasn't working. And he needed to hold her. He put his hands on her waist, about to pull her close, but she put her palms on his chest. Defensively. And, worse, she still looked disbelieving.

'I know you, Gabe,' she said, her voice harsh. 'You're a healer, not someone who hurts other people. You hate the thought of hurting someone. But I'm strong, I'm not like Diana, I'm not going to crumble.'

'You know, I bloody wish you would,' he said, tightening his grip on her and pulling her closer despite her hands blocking him. 'I wish you'd open up and tell me how you're feeling. It's okay to admit to being upset. It's okay to ask for help. It's okay to need something from someone.'

From *him*. He wanted her to want everything from him.

But she shook her head. 'When you were a kid you looked after the orphan lambs. I don't want to be another orphan lamb for you.'

'Roxie, you're not listening to me. I *know* how strong you are. The strongest person I've ever met. You're all steel, able to make whatever sacrifice necessary. So I don't feel sorry for you, I feel sorry for me having to try and match your courage. I don't think you're some orphan lamb who needs rescuing. Quite the opposite.' He was determined to prove it to her—even if it took him the rest of his life to wear her down enough to accept what he had to give. 'You're brave and terrifyingly independent. You learned how to load syringes so you could administer pain relief to the people you loved most. You cared for them, helped them, fought to give them the best chance. You grew that massive garden, filled with wonderful goodness, made all that food with such love. You put your own dreams on hold for so long and I know you did that gladly. And I know you said this was your time now—to have your adventures and fun. And I don't want to hold you back. I don't want to stop you doing the things you want to do. But I do want a place in your life and I'm going to fight for it, Roxie. I think you're blocking yourself from the biggest adventure of all, with *me*, and that's not true to *you*. You're an all-giving person.'

He could feel the constant tremors racking through her. Could feel her trying to stop them. To resist.

'I don't want to be,' she whispered.

And he heard the fear.

'You can't *be* any other way, and I want it for me.' He cupped her cheek and looked into the beautiful blue eyes that were filled with a hurt he ached to ease. If only she would give him the chance. 'And you deserve someone to give it all back to you too. That would be me.' He smiled. 'You're not meant to be alone. I felt the way you held me, Roxie, I felt that need in you and I hope like hell I'm not delusional on that. You know I never wanted to commit, never wanted to compromise. I thought I had my life plan perfect. But then I met you. And now? I'd do anything for you. So be with me. Lean on me. That's what people who love each other do.' He bent his head nearer, his heart hurting for hers. 'I'm sorry you lost your family. But you can't protect yourself from loving any more. That's not living. You, more than anyone, are supposed to love. You need your connections, your history. You need your home and I'm sorry if being with me there spoilt that place for you. Is that what happened?' He'd had the awful fear that he'd somehow ruined it for her.

'Oh, no,' she breathed, her eyes full of distress. 'I just couldn't bear it any more—everyone I loved I lost in that house.' She bit on her lip, then whispered, 'Including you.'

'You never lost me.' He lifted her face with gentle fingers. 'But don't leave me in the wilderness now, Roxie. I want you. I want everything with you.'

He swore he could see her heart reflected in those pure blue eyes—glistening, vulnerable, beautiful. And as he watched the smallest curve to her lips grew and she blinked—her gaze suddenly stronger, direct, true.

'Everything?'

That hint of undaunted tease, of Foxy Roxie, made his bones liquefy.

'The works,' he promised.

She moved closer, snuggling right against him. Gabe's blood fizzed as her fingers curled into his shirt. Holding him close now—she clutched as if she was never going to let him go. She rose on tiptoe, her heart bursting, and whispered, 'But you know I've got quite an imagination, right?'

'I can't wait to see what you're going to add to my list,' he breathed, bending to brush her lips.

'*You* have a list?' Her lips curved against his.

'Come with me now and I'll show you it,' he invited, then swooped.

Roxie's spirit soared to the heavens like a cork fired from a bottle of champagne. She lifted her hand, feeling his warm jaw with her cold fingers, holding his head to hers. Deep, yearning, passionate. Her tired eyes closed as he filled her senses, pouring warmth and love into her cold bones. She did as he'd invited—leaned on him, drawing on his heat and strength and heart. His arms tightened all the more around her, pulling her closer and closer.

'Please don't ever let me go again,' she muttered.

'Never.' He kissed her fear away. 'Come on, let's get some place else before we get arrested.'

He kept her close, tucked in right beside him as they walked to flag a cab. She wasn't letting him go either, one hand still curled into his shirt. 'Shouldn't you be helping the team prep for the next game?' she asked, once they'd gotten in the back of a taxi. Suddenly she was nervous of the future that only seconds ago had seemed easy and perfect. 'It's only early in the season.'

'I've got this one covered but, you're right, I can only stay a few days unless I resign.' His arm tightened around her shoulder as she tensed in rejection of that idea. 'I know you want to travel and I don't want to stop you doing that. So maybe I could come over every couple of weeks. Even for just a few nights. I can meet you wherever.'

Every couple of weeks? She vehemently shook her head. 'You can't fly all this way and back again all that often. You'll get too tired and it costs too much.'

He opened his mouth to argue but she pressed the backs of her fingers against it. Because no way was she being apart from him for that long.

'Maybe we could travel together for a while when the season ends.' She smiled when she saw his frown, pushed her fingers more firmly against his lips when she felt them move. 'I could come back and dance for the rest of the season. Even as just the substitute. I feel bad for running out on Chelsea.'

His eyes widened and the rest of him went very still.

'I want to come back with you,' she whispered. 'I don't want to do this trip on my own. I want to go to all

the fun places, but I want to do that *with* you. I'm not
letting *you* go either.'

He pulled her back into a tight embrace. She felt his
face, hot and hard pressed against her neck. He said nothing for a while. Didn't kiss her. Just held her close. The
way she needed to be held. His muscles bunched. What
she'd just said meant something to him. As she began
to understand that he really meant it. That he loved her
and wanted her. And, scared though she was, the beauty
and magic of it overruled that fear.

He pulled back and looked in her eyes. 'You know
I'm going to buy the Treehouse.'

'Oh, Gabe, I can't let you do that. It's not worth it.'
Her lawyer had been in touch, the offers from develop-
ers had started—an insane amount of money was on the
table because of the location.

'Then you'd better take it off the market and let me
use the money I would have spent buying it, fixing it. It
can be fixed. I love it and so do you. We're not letting it
go.'

The emotion bursting within her rendered her immo-
bile—so far beyond happy, she was speechless.

His smile just broadened. 'We'll get the tree fixed,
we can replant the garden and let the hedge grow back.'

She inhaled deeply and managed a nod. He cupped
her face with both his hands and drew closer to kiss her.
Kiss her and kiss her and kiss her.

Thanks heavens his hotel was a mere five-minute
drive from Covent Garden because in those few magic
minutes the cab's windows were fogged and she was
frantic to be alone with him.

'This is a bit flasher than my hostel,' she said vaguely,
blinking as they walked through the gleaming, posh
lobby.

'Wait 'til you see my suite,' he murmured, guiding her to the lift.

Anticipation shimmied through her veins.

He caught her eye; a wild look entered his. 'Just give me a chance to unlock the door, okay?'

She skipped alongside him, but once in the room he didn't stop by the massive bed—instead he led her the twenty steps further into the enormous en suite. And in the doorway, Roxie stopped—stunned.

The bath was huge, full of steaming water and billions of white, sparkling bubbles. There were soft scented candles lit, there was all indulgence to be had.

He caught her jaw-to-the-floor moment and winked. 'Know you like your bubbles.'

Indeed there were two champagne flutes on a tray, but Roxie's eyes were glued to the thing standing beside them. 'That's not a bottle, that's practically a keg.' She walked over to it, touching the dewy glass, the coldness assuring her this was all real—not her mind presenting the most incredible fantasy ever.

'You get kegs of beer,' he jeered lightly. 'That's a jeroboam. There are more in the fridge. For *my* list.'

His teasing talk kindled her own, easing her through the emotion of seeing the effort he'd gone to for her. 'Must be a massive fridge.' She'd never seen such a giant bottle of champagne.

He chuckled. 'I thought this was a better size for sharing.'

'Because you've invited the whole rugby team here?' She pretended to look around the room for the crowds. But less than a second later she sobered, because she truly couldn't believe he'd done all this. For her. 'How did you get this organised so quickly?' They'd only been in the hotel a minute.

Gabe reached into his pocket. 'I don't know if you've come across these things much, Roxie. They're called mobile phones.' He'd pulled out two of them—his and her silver-clad one.

Horrified, she stared at the two gadgets. And then she couldn't see them any more because her eyes flooded with tears denied too long. Rivers and rivers of tears.

The phones hit the floor with a clatter and in a second she was pressed tight against his hard strength.

'You're going to cry *now*?' he asked, aghast. 'Over a stupid phone?'

'Not the phone,' she sobbed. 'Because *I* was stupid. And scared. And I nearly lost my future as well as my past.'

His arms tightened more.

She cried more. 'You came after me. You found me. You love me.'

Oh, she believed it now. Needed it now. Was so happy she couldn't possibly hope to express it.

He thrust his fingers through her hair, massaging the base of her skull and tilting her head back to meet his kiss. Her whole body was one big shiver. He peeled the clothes from her, then pretty much ripped his own off. A haze of husky words, whispers of love and trust, promises, and touches that led to absolute ecstasy.

And many, many minutes later, even though her skin had been thoroughly warmed, it still tingled when she stepped into the bath. She stretched out and smiled at the sight of him opposite her, his glorious body half hidden in the mass of pearlescent froth.

'What if you hadn't found me at the ballet?' she asked, unable to bear the thought that he mightn't have found her. 'How many nights were you going to go there?'

'A few more, then I was going to bribe your lawyer

into giving me your address, or contact the embassy or something. Anything.'

'And what would you have done if I'd been fine? If I'd been off at a nightclub pulling some random guy?'

Gabe's dark eyes sharpened. 'I'd have punched his lights out.' But then his grin flashed. 'I told you I'd do anything, was totally up for a fight. But I never thought for a second you'd be off with someone else. Not you.'

'I was never going near another man,' she admitted. 'Too busy breaking my heart over you.' She'd been so stupid and scared. 'I should have said something to you.'

'You had to go,' he said softly. 'You'd been dreaming of it for so long, you had to go and see what if it was really what you wanted. I didn't want to try and stand in your way.'

Roxie's blood chilled, despite the warmth of the water. 'I knew I didn't want to go at the airport,' she admitted sadly. 'I couldn't turn away from you. But I didn't think—'

He stopped her rising distress by pulling her to him and planting a kiss so passionate and perfect that she knew there was such a thing as paradise on earth.

'Worst moment of my life,' he muttered against her skin. 'I really believed you wanted to go. But I knew right away I'd made an awful mistake. I should have gone with you then and there. Instead it took me four hours to get everything organised so I could follow you.'

She gave a watery chuckle and wrapped her legs around his waist, her arms around his shoulders, embracing him. In return he held her, caressed her, fulfilled her. She rested her head on his shoulder, at home.

'I love you, Gabe,' Roxie finally admitted. And in that instant, she'd never felt so free.

EPILOGUE

12 Months Later

HE WAS waiting for her when she came out to lock up. Her store had been open a month—dancewear supplies, costumes, theatre make-up, pointe shoes. At this stage she didn't stock nipple tassles but she knew Gabe held hope eternal.

Tonight they'd have their first night back at the Treehouse. It had taken months for the remedial work to be completed. They'd rented a small apartment nearby and Roxie had spent her days supervising both the repair job and the outfit of her store, her evenings choreographing new routines with Chelsea for the Blades. After the big digger work had finished at the Treehouse, she'd replanted the garden—not completely vegetables this time, but the occasional amazing flower as well. Now Gabe parked in the refurbished garage and with a flourish opened the front door for her. She literally danced in, so happy to be home.

'Oh, look, you have mail already.' He took the envelope pinned to the tree-trunk and handed it to her.

'Specially delivered.' She took it with a smile and a kiss that threatened to go wild—loving him so completely.

'Not yet.' He broke free and stepped back from her, his hands up in the surrender position. 'Open it first.'

She did and drew out the gilt card, reading the beautiful script. 'Tickets to the Paris Opera Ballet?'

'*Giselle*, of course.'

She was going to *Giselle*, in Paris, with Gabe? 'You mean you're coming with me?' She almost squealed, this day just couldn't get better.

'Nothing I like more in the world than coming with you.' He waggled his brows. 'And seeing we'll be in France, I've booked a trip to Champagne. To the House of Bollinger.'

'No,' she screeched. 'As in like the factory? Where they grow the grapes and bottle the bubbles?' That would be too much fun.

'Well, it is the only thing you drink,' he teased. 'But maybe we could try some others too—you know, Moët, Veuve, Taittinger? We could bubble around the region, don't you think?'

'Absolutely!' She wrapped her arms around him and squealed. 'That would be fantastic.'

He chuckled as he hugged her. 'I love you and I love this place.'

Oh, ditto, ditto, ditto.

She reluctantly eased out of his kiss. 'But there's still something wrong with the house you know,' she whispered, shyly hiding her face in his neck.

'What's that?' He waited, quiet, to catch her answer.

'There are only two bedrooms.' She leaned back so she could see into his eyes and took hold of some courage. 'I don't want to have an only child.'

His eyes widened and his arms tightened. 'You're pregnant?' He lifted her and twirled and positively shouted. 'Oh, darling, that's brilliant!'

'No!' She laughed, her heart soaring at his ecstatic response. 'I'm not pregnant *yet*. I just thought I might like to be. One day. More than once.'

He stopped spinning her, but kept his hold super tight as he lowered her to the ground. His eyes glowed, his growl of amusement warm, then he smiled the most heartfelt smile she'd ever seen. 'Roxie, you can have as many children as you want, whenever you want.'

Relief tumbled through her. 'Are you sure? You never wanted—'

'I was wrong about so many things I thought I didn't want. And I couldn't be happier about that.' He suddenly stepped back and tugged her hand. 'Though I have to admit, I'm just a little glad you're not pregnant right *now*, because I have something for you.' He led her to the kitchen.

She stopped in the doorway. 'What is *that*?' Her shoulders began to shake.

'A Nebuchadnezzar of Bollinger,' he answered drolly.

'A *what*?' she spluttered with laughter.

'A Nebuchadnezzar. Fifteen litres. Just *imagine* how many million bubbles.'

'A *gazillion* bubbles. Did you hire a crane to get it in here?'

'Yeah, because there are three of them—the others are in the bath. And this time I actually did invite the team to share it with us, as well as all the Blades. But they're waiting for my signal.'

'Really?' She glanced out of the kitchen window and saw the juvenile plants were festooned with fairy lights. 'Are you going to give them the signal?'

'In a minute,' he said deeply. 'Something to do first.'

She turned to look at him. He wound his arms around her waist and tugged.

'You know that trip to France?' he said. 'There are a couple of conditions.'

This time Roxie's heart soared so high so quick it broke the sound barrier. 'What conditions?' Oh, she was so breathy.

He held her so close, his eyes so full of love they made hers water.

'On *my* list, Roxie,' he whispered, bringing his face to hers. 'Before we have the babies, we have the wedding. And in between the two, we have the honeymoon. In France.'

There was only one thing she could say to that. 'Okay.'

'Okay?'

'Oh, yeah. That's really okay.' She laughed as much as she cried and then could manage neither as he kissed her—out of control, adoring, explicit.

'Did you really invite the team?' She tore her lips from his in part despair.

'For the engagement party. That's the thing on the very top of my list. That's tonight.' He breathed hard. 'But we could steal a few minutes before I sound the horn. Right?'

'Well, you always did like room for spontaneity,' she teased, inside totally desperate herself. 'Why not a few minutes now, then hours together after when they're gone—okay?'

'For *ever* after.' He smiled wickedly as he swept her in his arms and charged up the stairs to their room.

And Roxie knew the happiness bubbling inside her now was never, ever going to burst.

* * * * *

CLASSIC

EXTRA

COMING NEXT MONTH from Harlequin Presents®
AVAILABLE MAY 29, 2012

#3065 A SECRET DISGRACE
Penny Jordan

#3066 THE SHEIKH'S HEIR
The Santina Crown
Sharon Kendrick

#3067 A VOW OF OBLIGATION
Marriage By Command
Lynne Graham

#3068 THE FORBIDDEN FERRARA
Sarah Morgan

#3069 NOT FIT FOR A KING?
A Royal Scandal
Jane Porter

#3070 THE REPLACEMENT WIFE
Caitlin Crews

COMING NEXT MONTH from Harlequin Presents® EXTRA
AVAILABLE JUNE 12, 2012

#201 UNDONE BY HIS TOUCH
Dark-Hearted Tycoons
Annie West

#202 STEPPING OUT OF THE SHADOWS
Dark-Hearted Tycoons
Robyn Donald

#203 REDEMPTION OF A HOLLYWOOD STARLET
Good Girls in Disgrace!
Kimberly Lang

#204 INNOCENT 'TIL PROVEN OTHERWISE
Good Girls in Disgrace!
Amy Andrews

You can find more information on upcoming Harlequin®
titles, free excerpts and more at www.Harlequin.com.

HPECNM0512

REQUEST YOUR FREE BOOKS!

2 FREE NOVELS PLUS
2 FREE GIFTS!

YES! Please send me 2 FREE Harlequin Presents® novels and my 2 FREE gifts (gifts are worth about $10). After receiving them, if I don't wish to receive any more books, I can return the shipping statement marked "cancel." If I don't cancel, I will receive 6 brand-new novels every month and be billed just $4.30 per book in the U.S. or $4.99 per book in Canada. That's a saving of at least 14% off the cover price! It's quite a bargain! Shipping and handling is just 50¢ per book in the U.S. and 75¢ per book in Canada.* I understand that accepting the 2 free books and gifts places me under no obligation to buy anything. I can always return a shipment and cancel at any time. Even if I never buy another book, the two free books and gifts are mine to keep forever.

106/306 HDN FERQ

Name	(PLEASE PRINT)
Address	Apt. #
City	State/Prov.	Zip/Postal Code

Signature (if under 18, a parent or guardian must sign)

Mail to the **Reader Service**:
IN U.S.A.: P.O. Box 1867, Buffalo, NY 14240-1867
IN CANADA: P.O. Box 609, Fort Erie, Ontario L2A 5X3

Not valid for current subscribers to Harlequin Presents books.

**Are you a current subscriber to Harlequin Presents books
and want to receive the larger-print edition?
Call 1-800-873-8635 or visit www.ReaderService.com.**

* Terms and prices subject to change without notice. Prices do not include applicable taxes. Sales tax applicable in N.Y. Canadian residents will be charged applicable taxes. Offer not valid in Quebec. This offer is limited to one order per household. All orders subject to credit approval. Credit or debit balances in a customer's account(s) may be offset by any other outstanding balance owed by or to the customer. Please allow 4 to 6 weeks for delivery. Offer available while quantities last.

Your Privacy—The Reader Service is committed to protecting your privacy. Our Privacy Policy is available online at www.ReaderService.com or upon request from the Reader Service.

We make a portion of our mailing list available to reputable third parties that offer products we believe may interest you. If you prefer that we not exchange your name with third parties, or if you wish to clarify or modify your communication preferences, please visit us at www.ReaderService.com/consumerschoice or write to us at Reader Service Preference Service, P.O. Box 9062, Buffalo, NY 14269. Include your complete name and address.

HPI1B

Harlequin® Romance

A touching new duet from fan-favorite author

SUSAN MEIER

First Time **DADS!**

When millionaire CEO Max Montgomery spots
Kate Hunter-Montgomery—the wife he's never forgotten—
back in town with a daughter who looks just like him, he's
determined to win her back. But can this savvy business tycoon
convince Kate to trust him a second time with her heart?

Find out this June in

THE TYCOON'S SECRET DAUGHTER

And look for book 2 coming this August!

NANNY FOR THE MILLIONAIRE'S TWINS

Saddle up with Harlequin® series books this summer
and find a cowboy for every mood!

A Ferrara would never sit down at a Baracchi table for fear of being poisoned.

Fia had no idea why Santo was here. He didn't know.

He *couldn't* know.

"*Buona sera,* Fia."

A deep male voice came from the doorway, and she turned. The crazy thing was, she didn't know his voice. But she knew his eyes and they were looking at her now—two dark pools of dangerous black. They gleamed bright with intelligence and hard with ruthless purpose. They were the eyes of a man who thrived in a cutthroat business environment. A man who knew what he wanted and wasn't afraid to go after it. They were the same eyes that had glittered into hers in the darkness three years before as they'd ripped each other's clothes and slaked a fierce hunger.

He was exactly the same. Still the same "born to rule" Ferrara self-confidence; the same innate sophistication, polished until it shone bright as the paintwork of his Lamborghini.

She wanted him to go to hell and stay there.

He was her biggest mistake.

And judging from the cold, cynical glint in his eye, he considered her to be his.

"Well, this is a surprise. The Ferrara brothers don't usually step down from their ivory tower to mingle with us mortals. Checking out the competition?" She adopted her most businesslike tone, while all the time her anxiety was rising and the questions were pounding through her head.

Did he know?

Had he found out?

A faint smile touched his mouth and the movement distracted her. There was an almost deadly beauty in the sensual curve of those lips. Everything about the man was dark and sexual, as if he'd been designed for the express purpose of drawing women to their doom. If rumor were correct, he did that with appalling frequency.

Fia wasn't fooled by his apparently relaxed pose or his deceptively mild tone.

Santo Ferrara was the most dangerous man she'd ever met.

Will Santo discover Fia's secret?

Find out in THE FORBIDDEN FERRARA
by USA TODAY bestselling author Sarah Morgan,
available this June from Harlequin Presents®!

EXP0612

Live like royalty...if only for a day.

Discover a passionate duet from

Jane Porter

When blue blood runs hot...

When Hannah Smith agrees to switch places for a day with
Princess Emmeline, a woman who looks exactly like her, she
soon ends up in some royal hot water. Especially when Emmeline
disappears and Hannah finds herself with a country to run and
a gorgeous, off-limits king she's quickly falling for—Emmeline's
fiancé! What's a fake princess to do?

NOT FIT FOR A KING?
Available June 2012

And coming soon in July
HIS MAJESTY'S MISTAKE

Available wherever books are sold.

SPECIAL EDITION

Life, Love and Family

USA TODAY bestselling author

Marie Ferrarella

enchants readers in

ONCE UPON A MATCHMAKER

Micah Muldare's aunt is worried that her nephew is going to wind up alone in his old age...but this matchmaking mama has just the thing! When Micah finds himself accused of theft, defense lawyer Tracy Ryan agrees to help him as a favor to his aunt, but soon finds herself drawn to more than just his case. Will Micah open up his heart and realize Tracy is his match?

Available June 2012

Saddle up with Harlequin® series books this summer and find a cowboy for every mood!

Available wherever books are sold.

www.Harlequin.com

HSE65674